Stuffed Shorts

Sylvia Morrow

Marlon

by Sylvia Morrow

Content Warnings

♥

This story contains one brief occurrence of the *intended* assault of a sleeping child. The mention occurs in chapter **Two**-*Marlon.*

At the end of the content warnings, I will post a spoiler warning and then do a (very) brief summary of what happens in chapter two so that you can skip that if you want to.

The remaining content warnings:

Yes they do have a kid in this book but she's adorable, murder, stabbing, poverty conditions, needing to seek false identities, orphanage, kidnapping a child from abusers, non-human creature that looks and acts human, mention of car accident death, mention of parent death, multiple sexual activities, home school, shoulder wound, tentacle, light religious mentions, mentions of bugs and rodents.

Spoiler for **Two**-*Marlon:*

Charlie attacks a sketchy orphanage employee to protect Imani and ends up stabbing the man in the shoulder. Marlon finishes the man off with the death-suck. All three go to an off-grid cabin Charlie knows of to hide out. Marlon starts to feel weird from all the extra power in his blanket body.

Spoiler over.

Chapter One

Charlie

"Come on, baby. Hurry up. We can't slow down here."

I tug Imani's little hand harder than I intend to. Urgency turns my normally soft touch rough. It's not an ideal start to a life together.

But neither was the murder.

"I'm scared, Mr. Charlie. It's dark. We're not supposed to go outside when it's dark," Imani says in her scratchy little voice.

"This is a special exception, little one. You get to go to a home of your own. With me. And I decided to take you at night, so the other kids don't get jealous. Makes sense, right?" Hopefully she buys the excuse, at least for now. I had to get her away from the orphanage as fast as possible. There was no time for an explanation when I was getting her out the door. How could I explain that her teacher is now a killer, a kidnapper, and on the run. *Please forgive me.*

"I'm gonna live with you?" There's a hint of suspicion and a lot of hope in her voice. "Really?"

"Really. No more Saint Simeon's House. No more of those people ever again." My jaw clenches at the last words. *Those people.* The people who hurt her. The ones we're running from.

"I didn't like those guys," Imani says, the quiet darkness in her voice bringing tears to the corners of my eyes. *If only I had known sooner.*

"Neither did I. Here's my car. Let's get in. You have to sit in the backseat. I'm sorry I don't have a booster seat for you yet. This happened very quickly. I'll get one though. For now, just buckle up really well. Let's get you out of the rain." I help her into the car, though she's hesitant at first. Her parents died in an accident from what I've heard, though it happened when she was too small to remember. She'd been in that hellhole ever since. "It's okay. I'm a wonderful driver."

"Okay, Mr. Charlie." She's such a resilient little girl, letting me lift her into the car even with her fear. I buckle her in and force a smile as I pat her on the head. Her braids are matted, and most have lost their barrettes long ago. I'm going to fix her hair as soon as I can. "Can I have Marlon?"

"Of course, sweetie." I hand her the orange comforter which she named after a cartoon fish. She wouldn't leave the building without it. It's her prized possession. Before closing the door, I tuck it around her lap. Quickly, I make my way through the light rain to the other side.

"Alright, here we go." When I start the car, I drive away from the life I've lived for thirty years.

After what happened I can't take us to my home. Hell, I don't even know what happened really. It's all a blur. All I know is someone is dead, I'm decently sure I did it, and since I was the only one there, I'm in deep shit. *Pardon the language.* The sin that comes with murder is too heavy a weight on my soul to save myself, but I still must save the child.

I drive aimlessly until a thought strikes me. *The cabin. That's it.* My ex is a survivalist and has a cabin on his land that isn't technically supposed to exist. He isn't there most of the year. I'll drain my bank account of as much money as I can and head there. Hopefully this isn't the time of year he decides to vacation.

So that's what I'll do. Money. Cabin. We'll stay there and hope no one finds us. *We'll find a way out of this.* I'd do anything for Imani.

Chapter Two

Marlon

*O*ops. I didn't expect that to happen, but that man was going to hurt Charlie and Imani. What the heck else was I supposed to do? I would *never* let anyone hurt Imani.

But I feel weird now, all mixed up. When I drain living things, I sometimes get new emotions, or small abilities. I don't know how it works. When I touch things, I can just sort of suck the life from them, and it gives me a little boost. But this doesn't really feel like that. Maybe there was something in that man that's making me sick, darn it. He was a sick man, after all.

Imani was in her bed, sleeping quietly, and this awful man, who was meant to watch over her at night, took me off of her. She shivered but didn't wake up. I got real mad that he was making her cold, but there wasn't anything

I could do. And then he got this look on his face like he wanted to *really* hurt her. I couldn't do anything to stop him since I couldn't exactly walk over there and grab him. Charlie could though.

He wasn't even supposed to be there. Charlie works in the afternoons teaching the kids. Sometimes he comes in at nights when there's an emergency since he's got some kind of training. I don't understand it, I only know what I overhear when I'm with Imani. But tonight, I think he was just coming to get something he forgot. Darn lucky he was there too.

Charlie came in, saw what was happening, and grabbed that man. They started fighting. Really fighting! Like on the television Imani isn't supposed to watch, but the big kids put on sometimes anyway. There was kicking and punching and everything.

The bad man even took out a knife and was going to hurt Charlie with it. They both fell on the floor where the man had tossed me, right on top of me, and they were rolling around. Charlie and the man both had their hands on the knife. I got so darn mad I took all the energy I had from the dang bugs and mice in this nasty place and just grabbed hold of that man with my corners.

Charlie was too busy struggling to really notice I had hold of the creep. He took the knife easily when the man got surprised by me and he stabbed into the man's shoulder. The man was bleeding all over and shouting, trying to get up, but I held him down. I was still so darn mad I started sucking in the man's life force just like a cockroach.

He started shriveling up. Charlie jumped up all scared. I was pretty scared too, but I didn't stop. That man would hurt my friends if he got back up and I had to make sure he didn't. There was fear, panic, in Charlie's eyes, and he kept shaking the bad man, but I still didn't stop.

Pretty soon the man stopped moving. Charlie paced back and forth a bit before running his hands over his closely cropped hair. Soon he was waking up Imani and trying to get her to leave, but she wouldn't leave without me. Blood was all over me, but I shook off the stains and made myself clean. He looked surprised, but Charlie took me from under the shriveled up man anyway, and they both ran out of the building. Then we were in the car. Then eventually we got to the cabin.

And now I feel weird. I feel...*more*. I feel like I can't stop something changing in me and there's just no stopping it.

Chapter Three

Charlie

"I don't wanna go to bed," Imani says with a yawn. "I ain't even tired."

"You should say 'I'm *not* even tired' because school will start in less than a year and they'll want you to speak a certain way. Schools are strict like that." I brush her golden-brown cheek with my thumb as her eyes flutter closed.

She's laying in the only bed here, where we were sitting and talking about her favorite topic, tropical fish, but I don't want to move her. If I try to transfer her to the sofa where she's meant to sleep, she'll just wake up. I'll sleep on the sofa tonight.

"I don't want school. Wanna be with you," she whispers before finally settling into a light snore. I sit for a moment more to make sure she's fully asleep before heading to the living room.

The cabin is old, dusty, filled with cobwebs and mildew. But it's safe. At least for now. I can relax for a moment on the green plaid sofa. Relax as much as I can after I've watched a man shrivel nearly to dust in front of my eyes. *What have I done?* I drop my head into my hands and breathe deeply. There is nothing I can do now except sit. Sleep. Wait for a new day. With a sigh, I raise my head and flop backward on the sofa.

Some documentary on a red-haired former prince from a country I don't even live in is playing on the television. I start to switch it off but stop. May as well finish watching it. I need something to help me fall asleep.

I wrap Marlon, Imani's down comforter, around my shoulders. It's rare she would leave it anywhere. I contemplate bringing it into the room for her, but my comfort overpowers my kindness when I start to get warm.

As I continue to watch, I grow sleepier and sleepier. The blanket grows warmer and snugger around me. Snugger and snugger. Tight like a hug. A– What?

Groggily my eyes open and I awake fully to find myself cocooned in Marlon. *What the hell?* I struggle to move my arms, but they're held tight.

"Let go!" I shout but it's muffled by the fabric and feathers. "Let me out."

Suddenly, it does let me go. The blanket falls to the floor between the television and me. And it begins to...*pulse*. *Throb. Stretch.*

It's alive.

Chapter Four

Marlon

I feel like...I need to move. Something in me is changing and I don't think I can stop it anymore. When I'm feeling almost like I'm on the edge of a cliff, Charlie wraps me around him.

Charlie. He's so sweet. Lately I've started thinking about Charlie differently. I've noticed things about him I didn't used to. How nice his arms look when they flex. How full his lips are. How his skin is so beautifully dark that in some lights it almost looks blue. He's kind to all children. His voice is deep. He always tucks me in and never lets me fall on the floor. When I think about him, I feel good. *Really* good. I like Charlie.

When he falls asleep, I take my opportunity to hug him. I like to hug my people sometimes when they sleep, when they won't notice I act different from the other blankets, not that other blankets do any kind of acting. He feels *so darn good* that I can't help but squeeze him a little harder. But this time I can't stop. Even when he wakes up, I can't stop. Whatever is pushing me toward that cliff is starting to shove me off.

And then I fall.

I let go of Charlie, just barely, and fall to the floor, just in time to begin my change. Something happens to me, and I don't know what it is but it's big. In fact, as my fabric stretches, and feelings like lightning and acid run through me, I realize I'm not gonna be a blanket anymore.

I get this feeling like...like I have a choice to make. *What do I wanna be now?* And I think I have to make it fast. There's just too much power in me from draining that man.

A thought floats through the chaos in my mind. I wonder how much power would have been in him if Charlie hadn't stabbed him first? I shudder at the thought even as I pulse and stretch.

What do I wanna be? I wanna be with Charlie and Imani. But how?

I think I have to be a person, so I have to build a body. Oh boy. I'm glad I watched all those educational programs with Imani about anatomy.

Focusing hard, I begin to form arms and legs. *It's happening. I can feel them.* A torso. A head. There's still so much power.

Charlie is staring at me with his jaw dropped. He's not moving but he sure does look terrified. I think about how I must look. A person shaped blanket. That's not great. Must be real scary to look at.

On the television the red-haired man tells a story. Before I can stop myself, I begin to change, imitating the man on the screen. My arms and legs thin out, become more flesh-like. A suit and tie grow from my new body like leaves from a tree. I can feel my face changing, developing human-like features. *Oh gosh.*

When I feel everything stop moving around, I look Charlie right in the eyes. They're wide open, the deep, brown color nearly black with how big his pupils have grown.

"Well. I guess I'm not a blanket anymore. Can I still stay here?" I ask in a voice that sounds like a toy accordion filled with applesauce.

Charlie makes a garbled noise, then, eyes rolling backward, passes out.

Chapter Five

Charlie

*W*hat a wild dream. I must have–

"You're awake," a strained, scratchy voice says from a chair next to the sofa where I'm now laying. Someone must have laid me out here.

"Who the hell are you?" I ask as I sit bolt upright.

"No need for rude language now. It's just me, Marlon. Same as always," the familiar, handsome man in front of me says. Familiar from the television, not from real life, I realize.

"Same as always, my ass. I saw you do...something. What are you? An alien? A monster? A demon? Begone demon!" I form my fingers into the shape of a cross, but the man just frowns at me.

"I'm a blanket. Well, a man now. I think I used to be a bird. That's about it. What ya see is what ya get. Anyway, sorry about killing that man. I didn't mean to make you have to move away. He was gonna hurt Imani though so I'm not sorry I stopped him."

This is too much to take in at once. I drop my head into my hands and take several deep breaths. Finally, I focus on one point. My head snaps up, and I'm fully alert.

"You killed him? Not me?" I ask.

"Yep. Sucked the life right out of him. That's how I had the power to do this." He gestures to his new face and body. "It's like draining his battery and giving me the juice."

"That means I didn't do it. My soul is safe." I breathe a sigh of relief and sit back. "Still, no one would believe the story. If I tell them a blanket killed the man they'll only commit me to an institution and return Imani to Saint Simeon's. No, I cannot let her go back."

"Can't you just go somewhere else? Pretend to be someone else?" He scratches his head in thought.

What the blanket man said gives me an idea. Not a particularly legal idea, but an idea, nonetheless.

"Well, demon, we may have to do just that."

Chapter Six

Marlon

It's been a few months since the cabin.

Charlie has mostly gotten over the fact that I'm a blanket. Feather. Bird. Whatever. He still calls me a demon sometimes, but I think it's a joke. I hope. It was probably easier for him to accept what happened because he saw it go down. If I had just shown up when he wasn't looking, he'd probably have thought I was a regular human intruder or something, and things would have been a lot different. I'm glad it worked out though because we've been getting along swell.

Imani was disappointed to lose her blanket, but when she was told that I used to be said blanket she pretty much believed it right away. I don't know if she's just easy to convince or if it's because my skin is still made of fabric.

Either way, she's fine with it. I think she's mostly just happy to have two people who care about her around.

It took a little time, but Charlie did manage to find someone to make new identities for him and Imani, and a first one for me. Boy, was that guy sketchy. They just called him "Cadillac Dan" and we weren't allowed to talk to him. Just go, listen, leave. Got the job done though.

We had to stay in some pretty awful places and do some not-so-great things to get enough money for our first apartment, but we did it. We kept Imani safe and away from anything and anyone dangerous. I would never let her get hurt and I know Charlie wouldn't either.

I've had to learn more about life than just what was on kid's television pretty fast. I kind of miss seeing the world the old way.

All of the rough situations made us have to really learn to trust each other and we've really all grown pretty darn close. We're a real family now, even if we don't have blood connecting us.

When we finally settled down, Charlie decided to stay home with Imani and do her first couple years of school as home school, since we can't afford daycare, and after looking at finances it really was the best option out of some pretty terrible ones. So, I'm the one who has to work. I got a job at a big retailer stocking shelves, mostly in the home goods and bedding area. It's not so bad.

We don't have a lot, but we have each other at least. Someday we'll have more. Hopefully. Because our apartment could use some help. The appliances barely work, the hallways always smell like garbage, our lights flicker randomly, the hot water is a joke, the noise level outside is atrocious, and that's only the start. But I'm working hard to pay the rent anyway, and I'm happy we have a place to live at all.

Today I got home from work, and I was pretty tired. I don't get really physically exhausted unless I haven't taken sips of power from people in a while. I don't like taking sips from nice people, so I just stick to really rude customers. There's no shortage of those generally, but business has been a bit slow.

The springs on the old sofa squeal as I sit down and wrap my arms around my knees. I lay my head back against the cushions and close my eyes, just thinking about ways I can maybe make some more money for the household. I think about that a lot since I really want Imani to get the new scooter she talks about.

"Thinking about money again, demon?" Charlie asks from behind me in his deep, rich voice.

"You caught me. I'm thinking about maybe taking overtime in the café."

"No. You can't get wet. Your fabric will get all soggy." He shakes my arm reminding me of when I tried to do the dishes. It didn't go so well. Feather-stuffed fabric and water don't mix.

"You're right. As usual." I smile at him, showing the gap in my teeth he likes to joke about. "I just feel like things will never get better sometimes."

"Where I come from, they say 'Lu metti yàggul te ku muñ muuñ.' Whatever is painful does not last, and whoever perseveres smiles." He sits down, wraps one of his strong arms around me. When he mentions anything involving Senegal, the place he was born, I know he's comfortable, that he trusts me. I feel a warmth run through me that's more than just comfort. "We'll get through this. I swear it."

"Alright." I drop my head on his shoulder. He smells like shea butter lotion, crayons, and baby powder deodorant. His specific mix of scent always soothes me. "Want me to make you dinner?"

"I absolutely do not. You still cannot cook worth a damn. When Imani gets out of the bathroom you can play with her while I cook. You're much better at that."

"I'm gonna get better at cooking, I swear it. You're gonna want me cooking for you every day," I say with a determined grin.

"I'm happy to have you around every day either way."

Charlie's eyes soften, and for a moment I feel something pass between us. Something I don't really understand, but I'd like to.

"Marlon! You're home!" A voice squeals from the bathroom door.

"Flush the toilet!" I shout.

"Wash your hands!" Charlie shouts.

We both lean our heads back over the sofa and sigh.

Chapter Seven

Charlie

Things have gotten a little better. I've been able to take some work from home hours when not helping Imani, and Marlon has gotten a raise. We're careful with every dime and one day things will be great, I have faith.

Aside from money, life is wonderful. Imani is so smart, so sweet. We take her to the park and library as often as she wants so she can be with other children. The parents there assume Marlon and I are a romantic couple, and we let them think that. It's an easier explanation than the truth.

The truth...well, part of the truth is that I think there might be something developing between Marlon and me. I won't push it, however, because I don't know anything about what a blanket man feels romantically. Does he feel anything of the sort at all? I know *I* feel something.

He works so hard. A good work ethic has always been something important to me in a partner. No lazy layabouts for me. He smiles easily and genuinely. When I'm feeling down, I know his gapped teeth will lift me up. And he is very handsome, though in a strange way. If you would have told me I'd be attracted to a freckled man with demon-red hair a few years back I'd have laughed. Not even beginning to mention that there is a fabric texture to him that was shocking at first but that I've grown used to. It's part of him. And I think I'd like whatever he is. Whatever he looked like, or felt like, he'd still be Marlon.

"Hey there Charlie! You taking Imani to the pool to-day?" Marlon asks as he sees me exit the bedroom.

"No. She wants to go to the playground. More dirt and sand to clean from her shoes. I'm so joyful."

Marlon laughs with a shake of his head. "Tonight, when Imani goes to bed can I please try to cook for you again? I'm trying my darndest, I swear."

"Trying to poison me, demon? Well, you know I'm too strong for your potions. Bring it on." I laugh.

"Excellent! I swear it's gonna be great this time!" He's practically bouncing in his seat now. For his sake I hope it is good. I will not lie to him, and I don't want to hurt his feelings.

"Some strange person at work gave me a map, by the way. Do you know anything about this?" He hands me a much-folded piece of paper with an unlabeled map on it.

"I don't know. Somewhere in Bolivia. Perhaps Argentina. It's hard to tell from the way this is drawn. Who gave it to you?"

"They were really weird, but they said it was important. I should probably just toss it but, I don't know, I have a feeling I should keep it." His brow crinkles in thought.

"Then keep it. Don't overthink it. We have better things to do." I could think of many things I'd like to do with Marlon that would be a lot of fun.

Today at the playground we sit together on the bench and watch the children play. The parents all know us and wave hello as they pass. It's a beautiful day.

"Hey you two!" A blonde lady we see often named Maggie comes up to us waving. "How are you?"

"We're fine and dandy! And yourself?" Marlon replies.

"I'm great! We're just leaving but I had to say hi to y'all first. You're the absolute cutest couple I know, and you always make me smile. So gosh darn cute. Well, y'all have a nice day now. Bye!" She waves and turns back to her gaggle of children and muscular husband.

After a beat Marlon turns to me and asks, grin wide and blue eyes sparkling, "Do you think we'd make a cute couple, Charlie?"

I cough at the unexpected question, but I take the words as seriously as the feelings. "Yes, I suppose I do."

"Me too."

Things are very quiet between us the rest of the trip to the playground.

Chapter Eight

Marlon

"And here ya go. Steak, mashed potatoes, and green beans. I know it's not a fancy recipe but I tried to make something basic so I could really get the technique down. Anyway, I hope you like it," I say as I set the plates down in front of Charlie.

I wring my hands as I sit in my own seat across the table. Cooking has not been a talent of mine. Since I can't really taste anything, and the thought of eating honestly kind of disgusts me, it's hard to guess whether or not something will taste alright. I try to follow recipes but somehow, they always turn out wrong, darn it.

This time I tried really, really hard. I even recalibrated the junky old stove to make sure the temperature would be correct for baking the apple pie. Now Imani's in bed and I can finally give Charlie the food I've been working on. Gosh, I hope he likes it.

Charlie smiles wide and shimmies in his seat. None of our dining table chairs match but that's alright. A place to sit's a place to sit.

"It certainly is pleasing to the eye, Marlon. I want you to know that whether it tastes fine or not, I appreciate your efforts."

"Oh, just try it already. I'm on the edge of my seat."

Charlie barks out a laugh before picking up his knife and fork and cutting into the steak. The inside looks pink and tender. He nods as he lifts the meat to his mouth for a bite. When he begins to chew, his eyes close and a smile forms on his lips. He swallows, opens his eyes.

"You've done it. It's perfect." He rushes to take another bite as I stand, pumping my fist in the air.

"Woo!" I shout. "Finally!"

I start to head toward the kitchen, walking past Charlie as I go. He reaches out and grabs my elbow as I start to pass him.

"Stop. Where are you going?" he asks.

"To do the dishes. Then when you're done, I'll bring out dessert," I say matter of factly. It should be obvious to him. Doing the dishes is a chore I do often. It's fine as long as I wear the dish gloves. The time I forgot wasn't great. Soggy, floppy hands. Ugh.

"Please, sit while I eat. The dishes can wait. We have so little time to talk these days. I miss it." His brown eyes seek my blue ones and when they find them, they don't let go.

"Well, alright. But if they get all dry and crusty then you're doing them," I mumble.

"I don't mind." He laughs.

I sit and watch as he takes a bite of the potatoes with a smile, clearly enjoying them. My chest puffs with pride at my success.

"Has anything new happened lately, Marlon?"

"No, same old nothing. How about you?"

"Nothing here either."

There's quiet between us. Our silence has never been awkward before, but somehow it is right now. I speak again just to fill it.

"Imani got gum on that weird map earlier and tore a piece already. I swear I can't be trusted to take care of anything." I huff and shake my head.

"You've taken great care of our daughter. She knows she is loved and protected. Nothing is more important than that." There's a fierceness in Charlie's eyes, though his words are soft. He takes another bite and sits back further into his chair.

"That still sounds so strange to me. 'Our daughter.' Like we're a couple." I laugh softly but when I look at Charlie he isn't laughing. There is silence again but this time it isn't awkward, it's heavy. It's waiting. He sets his silverware down, leans forward.

"We could be a couple, Marlon. Could we not?" he asks quietly.

I pause to consider my answer carefully. It's not as if I haven't thought about this. I've thought he was beautiful since I was a blanket, for goodness' sake. And there's a clear connection between us. But there's a kid involved here. Things aren't easy.

"I mean…what if it doesn't work? I don't want to lose you and Imani."

"I would never take you away from Imani. She loves you too much. Even if I grew to hate you, I could never take you from her. Trust that." Charlie leans forward farther to grasp my hand over the table. He rubs his thumb along the back of my hand, and I feel secure as I'm caressed.

I think on it for a moment before nodding. I do trust that he'd never take her from me. I do trust *him*.

"But do you really want to be with *me*, or are you just bored and lonely?" I ask as the thought creeps into my mind. He could just want me out of desperation, a desire for romance he can't fulfill any other way. But I want to be truly wanted by him. It's important to make this distinction. I know that we've been stuck together a while, and I want to make sure he doesn't want me only because we're the last two stranded on our island. I can't help wanting a one true love when I was raised on cartoon romances, I suppose.

"Marlon. I do not make decisions lightly. When I do things, I do them with all my heart. I would not ask you to be mine if I did not want specifically you. *You,* Marlon. I want to feel your strange fabric skin against my own. If that is not something you want as well, then I will not offer again. I promise to leave you be and to return to how we were if you do not want me. But I must let you know now that you are what I want."

My mouth opens and closes several times silently before finally shutting. I nod my head rapidly.

"Yes. Yes, I want that. Us. I want us," I say, my words fumbled and awkward but understandable at least. I know they're understandable anyway because Charlie springs from his seat and walks toward me the few steps it takes to cross the distance between us. He drops to one knee, holds me on either side of my face, presses his mouth to my ear.

"Thank you, demon. I am blessed to have you."

And then he kisses me. My first kiss.

At first, it's just a press of his soft lips against my fabric ones. A shiver runs through my feather-filled body. I think *this is perfect* but then his warm, wet tongue glides across the seam of my closed lips and I know it's about to get even better.

I open my mouth a little and his tongue pushes in, forcing me to open even further. I moan at the feeling of being breached, being entered by someone. This is new, this is wonderful. I want *more*. I want *everything*.

I wrap my arms around Charlie's sides, pulling him closer to me as our kiss grows deeper, wilder. His hands explore my hair, running his fingers through the soft layers, gently tugging in a way that makes my eyes roll back under the lids. When I go to pull up the bottom of his sweater, he pulls away from me, takes the sides of my face again.

"That's far enough for tonight. We'll sleep and then tomorrow see if we feel the same, before we go further. Yes?" He looks me over, inspecting me for any doubt. I have none but appreciate his concern.

"I know I'll feel the same but if it makes you more comfortable then I'll wait. I'd wait for you forever, Charlie."

He presses his forehead against mine for a moment before pulling back, planting a kiss in the center of it, then standing up.

"I have dinner and apparently dessert to finish. Delicious too. I'm sure it's gotten cold by now, but the flavor will still be there." He smiles. I can't help but smile back.

We're a couple now.

Chapter Nine

Charlie

Sleep was difficult. I offered to sleep next to one another, but Marlon insisted on sleeping on the sofa like he normally does. He said he would not be able to rest if he were next to me. I agreed but it turns out I can't rest anyway.

The kiss between us has changed everything. It was truly magical. His tongue was so strange, but I didn't mind it. He could have been made of wood and I wouldn't have minded, because it's *him*. I've got it bad, as they say.

This morning, he left for work as usual, and I taught Imani. We are so lucky to have her, so I hope she is alright with Marlon and I being a couple, and not only friends, if she even understands the difference. Perhaps I should find out.

"Imani. Do you know the difference between a boyfriend and a friend that is a boy? Or a girlfriend and a friend that is a girl?" I ask as we play with stacking blocks during her recess time.

She purses her lips in thought before answering. "One is kisses and one is no kisses. Can I have the blue block? I want to make a tornado."

"A blue tornado? That's pretty creative there, little one. I can't wait to see it!" I hand her the brick as I smile. I suppose kisses and no kisses is good enough for now.

When Marlon gets home, we head to the park. We sit closer on the bench than ever as we talk.

"Anything new happen at work today?" I ask.

"Yes, actually. I'm pretty excited about it. I was going to wait until we were at home to tell you but it doesn't look like anyone can hear us, so I'll tell you now." Marlon looks around, I'm assuming to double check that no one is within hearing distance, then turns back to me. He says softly, "I have a brother. I met him today."

My eyebrows shoot up in surprise. *A brother?*

"I thought you were the only one! There are more? Is every feather on the bird going to be a man?"

"Whoa whoa." He holds his hands up in a stop gesture. "Slow down. I don't really know much other than we were two feathers that dropped. We *think* we're the only two from that bird. We talked a little on my break and he was very interested in that map from that weird guy. I'm gonna lend it to him. Gosh, can you believe it? A brother."

Before I can even comprehend the implications of such a thing, Imani skips up to us, braids bouncing as she goes.

"I wanna go home now. I'm hungry. Can we have pancakes?" she asks.

"Sure, little one. But I think Marlon should cook. Don't you think so, Marlon?" I raise my eyebrow at him teasingly, smiling at his frightened expression.

"I don't know if I can handle pancakes yet. Maybe I'll just cut up some fruit and pour the juice. Charlie can do the pancakes." If he was human, he'd be sweating right about now.

I grin widely and wrap my arm around his shoulder. "We can work together then."

I cook the pancakes while Marlon makes a fruit salad on the counter next to the stove. It's a small kitchen so we're very close to one another. I don't mind one bit.

"Look at this grape! It's perfect." Marlon holds up a particularly impressive looking purple grape.

"Ah, you should give it to Imani." I flip a pancake and offer him a smile.

"Nope. It's for you. Open wide." Marlon points the grape in my direction as I scoff.

"Don't feed me fruit, demon. We know what happens when your kind feed humans fruit." I love to joke with him about this sort of thing. He really doesn't even understand the references but plays along anyway. Such a good sport.

"Oh come on now, put it in your mouth," he says.

I feel my cheeks grow hot and it's not from the stove.

"Are we still talking about grapes, Marlon?" I ask with a raised brow.

Marlon looks confused for a second before his eyes grow wide. He turns back to cutting fruit silently. I laugh quietly to myself.

After dinner and bath time Imani heads to bed. The apartment is quiet, aside from the normal street noise and sirens in our less than desirable neighborhood. Marlon is putting away the last of the dishes when I walk behind him and put my hands on his waist. I gently press my body against his, run my nose along the back of his neck. He shivers and lets out a soft breath.

"Marlon. Come to bed with me tonight."

"I'd just keep you awake," he replies, his voice breathier than usual.

"I don't plan on sleeping with you there, demon. Not if I get my way." I slide my hand from his waist to his hairless stomach, down to the waistband of his corduroy pants. A snap breaks the silence when I pop the button there. "Do you understand?"

"Y–yes," he stutters. "I just–I don't know what I'm doing. I don't even know if my, uh, parts will be acceptable to you."

"I'll teach you. I care for you. We'll figure things out together. Come now, to the bedroom." I take his hand and softly tug in the direction of my room. A second passes before Marlon turns and nods.

"Alright," he says shakily. "Just don't blame me if things get weird."

Chapter Ten

Marlon

As soon as Charlie closes the door behind us, he wraps his strong arms around me and gives me the deepest kiss yet. The cock I built myself recently swells in excitement and I groan at the feeling. I don't know why I waited so long to make myself one. I experimented with it last night and *wow* does it feel nice. But with how just being like this with Charlie feels so good already I can tell it's going to get even better than it was alone.

Charlie backs me into the bed until I'm lying on it with my legs off and tugs off my old t-shirt. With great anticipation of the feeling of his skin on mine, I watch as he removes his own. When he leans down to kiss me, and we press together, that feeling is just as good as I imagined.

Next, he takes off his pants and undergarments. My eyes grow wide at the sight before me. He's beautiful. All lean muscles and dark, glistening skin, with the slightest roundness to his belly. He strokes his cock and a bead of pre-cum appears on the tip of it. A shaky breath escapes me. Charlie lurches forward suddenly and with one smooth motion tugs my pants to my ankles, revealing the cock I've made for myself.

His eyebrows raise when he sees what I've made. I'm nervous. Clearly, he hates it. I'll have to change it. It's horrible. It's–

"Fucking hell, it's huge," Charlie mumbles.

"Oh," I reply while he strokes himself, looking me up and down with heat in his eyes. "Is it alright? Should I change it?"

"It's fine, demon. Touch yourself. I want to see you stroke your cock for me."

I swallow the lump in my throat and do as he says. His breathing increases to a rapid pace as he watches me intently. His eyes are focused so strongly on me it makes me nervous, but also makes me feel attractive, more confident somehow at the same time.

"You look so fucking good with your big, fat cock in your hand. Lay down on the pillows," Charlie commands. I would do anything he tells me to do.

I lay flat on my back and Charlie lays his body on top of me, kissing me hard and grinding his hips against mine.

It feels so good and so right to be with him. I don't know why it's taken us so long.

"Your mouth is wonderful, Marlon. So strange with your satin tongue. I wonder how it would feel wrapped around my cock?" he practically purrs in my ear. It's a statement but also a suggestion, a request.

"Maybe we could find out," I reply in a whisper. "I don't know what I'm doing though. So just...cut me some slack if I fuck up."

"There's no fucking up," Charlie laughs, "unless you use teeth. Don't use teeth."

"I won't." I laugh in return. *No teeth. Got it.*

Charlie flips over onto his back and I crawl until I'm on my hands and knees over his body. *Oh gosh am I nervous.* I move down until I'm in the right position and take hold of his beautiful brown cock. *Alright. Here we go.*

The first taste surprises me. It's sort of salty and bitter at the same time. Now, I don't really taste much, and what little I do I don't generally like, but I kind of like this. What it says about me that the only flavor I like is human, I don't know, but it can only be something creepy. So, I don't think about it too long.

I lick along the head, the shaft, getting used to the feeling in my mouth before I wrap my lips around it. The way I begin to move seems to be okay if I'm judging by the noises

Charlie is making. He's hissing and sighing delightfully. I want to impress him, make him feel better than he's ever felt, so I decide to do something crazy.

I decide to use my abilities. My ability to change my form that is. I know it's risky, but I think it will pay off. So, I look him dead in the eyes and as I'm moving up and down, licking and sucking, I stretch my tongue out longer and longer until it's wrapped around his cock several times. I swirl it around, squeezing, finding every movement that makes him groan and repeating it until he's shouting and shooting loads of hot cum onto the back of my throat.

When he finishes, I retract my tongue to its normal size and sit up with a smile. Charlie lays there, panting, with a confused look on his face.

"What just happened?" he pants out.

"I can choose my shape, remember?" I say with a wide grin. "I just happened to decide on a little longer tongue than normal."

"A little?" He lets out one incredulous laugh. A moment passes while he stares at me in awe before he speaks again. "We're going to have a lot of fun."

Chapter Eleven

Charlie

"So, you can do any part?" I ask in shock.

I feel a tickle on my stomach, like a snake slithering around. I look down to see what was a beautiful cock is now a long, pointed tentacle. I jump with a startle, but still, I reach for it, stroking along the smooth, PVC-like texture.

"Well, that's certainly new."

"Yeah." He laughs. "This is kind of fun."

"Feel free to experiment all you like. What's mine is yours to explore," I softly chuckle.

The tentacle returns to the original shape. "I think I just want to try things the old-fashioned way tonight if that's okay. We can continue getting weird another time."

"Fine with me." I brush some ginger hair back from his pale brow. "Get on your back again. We'll come together this time."

As he does what I say I open the side table drawer and grab the bottle of lube. My cock is already hard again as I hover over him, spreading the lube on both our cocks. His eyelids flutter beautifully as I stroke him. I lay my body down onto his and kiss him, softly and deeply.

I hold both our cocks and begin to pump into my hands, stroking us, encouraging Marlon to move his hips as well with mine.

"Don't come until I tell you it's alright. We have to come together this time. Got it?"

"Okay. I think." His voice is strained but I can tell he's trying his best to agree.

"Good boy," I say against his lips, and he moans right as I sink my tongue into his mouth. Guess he liked that.

Soon we're frantically moving, and I can feel my orgasm approaching. The desperate look on Marlon's face says he can't hold back much longer.

"Alright. You can let go," I say, my forehead pressed against his.

I lose it first. A spray of sticky cum coats our hands and Marlon's chest, his stomach. I'm barely finished when

Marlon's hips raise, a loud groan escapes him, and he stiffens. Then, something highly unusual happens.

I bark out a laugh of surprise as a shower of soft, white, feathers float down in front of my face. Most of the time I don't think about the fact that Marlon started off as a comforter, but I suppose I must be reminded sometimes. I fall forward in laughter and kiss him over and over. He soon joins in, and we're wrapped in each other's arms, smiling and laughing for long minutes before we stop in sighs.

"I forgot to warn you about that," Marlon says with a sheepish look on his face.

"I think it's better you didn't. It was a great surprise." I lay my head on top of his and pull the blanket over us. "I can clean up the mess. Then I'll shower. You...do whatever it is you do to get clean."

"Oh, I insist on cleaning up the feathers. It's my mess."

"We can take turns then. There will be many opportunities in the future. I hope." I stroke my thumb along his cheek.

"I hope so too."

A knock comes at the door and Marlon and I look at each other in panic before it opens wide. Imani is standing there in her little pink nightgown, looking sleepy.

"I heard laughing." She looks at both of us appraisingly. "Were you kissing? Are you boyfriends now?"

"Well, you see, Marlon and I love each other very much," I say. I'm nervous as hell and have no idea where to go from here.

"Okay. You can be boyfriends. Don't wake me up though that's rude." She yawns and closes the door.

I hear her tiny feet slapping against the floor on the way back to her room and when it goes quiet, I let out a long breath and fall back down to the mattress.

"We love each other?" Marlon asks, laying his head on my chest. The beat of my heart must be so loud now I'll be surprised if he keeps his hearing.

"Do we not?" I ask back, a nervous shake to my words.

"Yeah, we do."

"Good." My heart slows, relaxing with the knowledge of my perfect destiny. "I have defeated the demon with the power of love. How predictable."

Chapter Twelve

Marlon

"Yep, my brother invited us to dinner. It's exciting! I've only met him a few times and it was always brief. He's an odd fellow, really. Kind of creepy, if I say so. But I think he's harmless. And he's my brother so we have to go! We're going to meet his family. I'm so excited! I can't wait!"

I'm practically bouncing on my toes as I tell Charlie the news. My brother Ori came into my work today to ask me to dinner to meet his family. Apparently, he's told them all about me and they're excited to meet me. I can't believe it! For a bit there I thought he was only using me for that darn map, and I'd never talk to him again.

"Are you sure about this? He's not going to turn us into the police or harm Imani or anything? We have to be careful, you know." Charlie is always worried. I understand. I also would do anything to protect Imani.

"As far as I know he doesn't know anything about what happened at the orphanage. And I really don't think he'll hurt us. He's just weird. Like, sort of dramatic. It'll be fine. We can go, right?" I put on my best puppy dog eyes and hope it works. It does.

"Fine. But if things seem off, we leave."

"Of course! You got it!"

"What's he got?" Imani asks, looking up from her book. She's still so little but she's reading way ahead for her age. Such a smart girl.

"Oh, he agreed to let us meet your uncle. My brother. His name's Ori. He's a little weird but he's got a family and we're gonna get along, I just know it."

Imani perks up. "Does he got kids?"

"Does he *have* kids," Charlie corrects. Imani and I both ignore him.

"I don't think so. Sorry, little buddy. But I think he's got a wife or girlfriend or something so at least it won't be all boys around for once."

"Well, that's good at least I guess." She goes back to reading her book and I turn back to Charlie.

"So, dinner with Ori then?" I ask.

He sighs and crosses his arms.

"I guess we're having dinner with Ori."

The Phoenix and the Goose

by Sylvia Morrow

THIS IS NOT A ROMANCE. THERE IS NO HAPPILY EVER AFTER.

I need to make it clear that this story is a **TRAGEDY**, not a romance. It will end with the death of both main characters. This is not a spoiler, as the basic plot has already been explained in "**Stuffed**." However, **you must know the basic characters and summary of this story to best enjoy the final "Stuffed" story, "Stuffed Up."** I will post a page that contains an **entire summary** of the story for those that want to know what happens in the story, but do not want to read it because of the content warnings. This way you can be caught up for the remaining stories.

The story also contains parts that require major content warnings. You may not want to read this story if you only want to read uplifting stories where the main characters

have happy endings, no animals are harmed, and no one is
a liar or a cheat.

Content Warnings

♥

Cheating, pet harmed, animal (not pet, not on page) death, death of main characters, no happily ever after, main character gets badly injured, awful death, sex, kidnapping, murder, burned alive, loved one being eaten, description of how an animal is butchered.

Spoilers

♥

Entire Plot Spoiler For Those That Want to Skip

This is for people who want to skip this novella due to triggers but want to continue with this series.

Do not read if you want to read this story. It contains FULL spoilers of the ENTIRE Phoenix and the Goose novella.

Again, **if you don't want spoilers, skip this** and go to Chapter One.

Summary:

Luke is a phoenix shifter. Phoenix shifters all come from Greece, but most moved to Texas. Some phoenixes have strong abilities to change their own and others' physical attributes, even into entirely different species. Luke has a fiancée named **Iris** who has that ability.

Luke did not choose to become engaged to Iris. The people in charge of the phoenixes—the Council—forced Luke and Iris together because of their strong bloodlines. Iris is a cruel person, who is determined to be on the Council, and Luke doesn't like her.

Luke meets a human named Lara. Despite knowing he shouldn't do it, he goes on a date with her. When he kisses her, he realizes she's his fated mate. Luke goes to the Council and tells them that he has to break his engagement with Iris because he has found his True Love.

The Council warns Luke that Iris is powerful and could react poorly to the breakup. The Council insists he must be certain that Lara is his True Love before they will agree to the breakup and gives him one week to think things through, during which he cannot tell Iris. Luke agrees.

After the meeting, Luke has a date with Lara where she really falls for him. They make love. The next day when she is working Luke comes into her job, not knowing that is her shop. She says she misses him after their date and calls him a "silly goose." She doesn't notice Iris there with him.

Upon discovering Luke has been cheating, Iris turns Lara into a goose and traps Luke in his phoenix form. Iris kidnaps them. Lara escapes out of Iris's car window but is injured when she lands on the highway. A goose farmer finds Lara and takes her to use for feathers and meat.

Luke escapes the car a while after Lara and searches for her. By the time he finds her, she's too injured to walk or fly away. Men on the farm capture Luke. While he is tied up, they kill and eat Lara.

Luke decides he cannot live without Lara and burns himself up, deciding not to be reborn out of the ashes. Before he burns up, two of his feathers get snagged on a rusty pole and float toward the barn where Lara's feathers are. The feathers are mixed with those of geese and made into a pillow and blanket.

Chapter One

Lara

Goosebumps travel up my bare arms as I stroll past the glass doors of the frozen foods aisle. It's cold in the freezer section. Hot as the blazes of hell outside, though. That's summer in Texas for you.

"Grab some pizzas, girly. I don't feel like dealing with delivery and all that tonight," my cousin says as she starts to walk away back to the beginning of the aisle. "Let me get some of those little cinnamon bread things."

"You got it, Vera."

Shivering, I open a door and grab a couple of pizzas as fast as I can, toss them in the cart, and hurry along. This is the last of the frozen food aisles and then we just have to grab a few things I forgot earlier, like beans. Can't leave the beans behind. When I speed around the corner, however, my trip to the legumes is delayed when I slam into an unexpected barrier.

"Oof."

A man clutches his stomach at the far end of my cart, his basket and its contents clattering to the floor.

"Oh! I'm so sorry! Are you alright? Let me help you with that."

I hurry to the side of the poor man I've just charged straight into and drop to the ground to pick up his goods. He crouches down to join me.

"It's okay, you don't have to. I'm sure it was an accident. Wait, was it an accident? If not, you should definitely help because that would be really mean, crashing into someone on purpose."

I pause with my hand halfway to picking up a bag of habanero peppers, checking his expression to make sure he's kidding. The sparkle in his strangely copper-colored eyes and the twitch to his full lips give him away.

"Yeah, I should help, then. I really have it out for cute blond guys. My apologies."

He really is cute. And I'm a flirt. Always have been.

I can tell by the way his lips roll in and his cheeks turn pink that he's trying not to laugh as he picks up a large jar of cinnamon sticks.

"Well, it's only mean to crash into the cute ones. The ugly ones are fair game," he says in an overly serious tone.

"Oh, of course, of course." I pick up a bag of what has to be nearly two pounds of fresh ginger root. "You have some very interesting groceries, Blondie."

"You went with Blondie? Damn. Was hoping for Cutie."

This time, he can't keep his laugh in once mine escapes.

"Alright, Cutie it is."

"What can I call you?" he asks, cheeks now turning even pinker against his fair skin.

Aww, he's shy.

"You think you're the only one who likes being called cute?" I give him a wink that has him shaking his head and smiling broadly. "But my name is Lara."

"Okay, Cute Lara. Nice to meet you. My name is Luke."

"Nice to meet you, Luke."

We shake hands, which seems awkwardly formal. It feels like I've known this guy forever, not just met him.

"You sure you're okay? I hit you pretty hard. I feel terrible." I cringe.

"It's alright, really. It was just a bump. Accidents happen."

He smiles so brightly and my heart flutters around the room, cartoon-style. After having been in so many relationships with people who wanted to hold every mistake over my head forever, *'Accidents happen'* is a really nice thing to hear.

"I have to run, but do you...do you want to talk again sometime? Not at the grocery store?" he asks as we stand.

I have to admit, I'm caught off guard. It's not like I've never been asked out before, but this blushing sweetie didn't seem like the type to make the first move. I'm certainly intrigued.

"Yeah, that would be great! Here, take my number."

We take our phones out and I tell him mine; he tells me his. There's a lot of nervous tucking my hair behind my ear on my end, despite being so brave just a moment before. I discover his nervous tic is rubbing the back of his neck. Despite the nerves, our smiles show how excited we both are.

"I look forward to seeing you soon, Lara."

"Same, Cutie."

And with that, we part ways. I'm off to check out the beans and he's off to the registers.

"Cutie, huh?" A moment later Vera meets me. She drops the frozen cinnamon bread in my cart. "Don't tell me you're gonna go out with that guy."

"Eh, I might."

Vera snatches the beans out of my hands and looks me in the eye. "You're supposed to be taking time off of dating."

"Don't worry. This one seems sweet. And I promise, I'll be gone at the first sign of trouble."

Chapter Two

Luke

"Luke? Hello? Earth to Luke!"

My sister tosses a balled-up napkin that hits me square in the forehead, interrupting my spinning thoughts about Lara. It's for the best. I *really* shouldn't be thinking about her. Not that I can stop. She's been the only thing on my mind since she slammed into me with her shopping cart.

But I really shouldn't have asked her out like I did. We can't have a future together, and it's crazy to even imagine one after one meeting. I shake my head, try to clear my thoughts.

"What's going on?"

"I asked why you're zoning out today."

I don't know, Emily, maybe because I met the girl of my dreams at the grocery store and I can't stop thinking about her even though I have a fiancée.

"Just tired. Eat your food, Emily."

My eyes flick to her plate, mostly empty compared to mine. Normally I'd gobble up the meal, a classic phoenix dish made from ginger, cinnamon, ghost pepper, anise, horseradish. The kind of stuff that would leave most humans panting.

"Well, wake up. Iris is coming over tonight and I'm not going to entertain her for you. She gives me the creeps."

Inside, I groan. I'd forgotten about that. She wanted to come over and discuss wedding colors. As if I care what our wedding decor looks like. I don't even want to marry her in the first place.

Iris is from a wealthy, healthy phoenix family. I'm considered lucky to be paired off with her—my family is middle class at best. There are only so many acceptable matches with how few phoenixes are left in the world, so to be paired off at all is a blessing. The leaders decided she and I would make good offspring, so we're getting married. That's that. I will do my duty for my species—even if I really don't want to.

"Make sure to keep your dog in your room," I grumble.

Iris hates dogs. *Really* hates dogs. I'm a fan of animals, but I don't think we'll be having pets when Iris and I are married. I saw what she did to a street cat who scratched her once and it wasn't pretty. Not willing to take a risk by putting an animal in a house with her.

There are a lot of reasons I wouldn't have chosen Iris as a wife on my own and that's one of them. But what the Council says goes. They want another healthy generation of phoenixes and they want Iris and me to be their breeding pair. It's depressing if I think about it too much so I just kind of...don't.

I suppose the "not thinking" is what got me in trouble with Lara. Then again, maybe it was too much thinking. Because I just *cannot* get her out of my head.

I finish eating my dinner and head to the shower. My mind wanders back to the woman at the grocery store today. When I saw her it was as if everyone else was in shadow but she lit up like a Christmas tree. All of that deep, tan skin showed off in her tiny shorts. Big, brown eyes, wrinkled at the edges with mischief. Crayon-red curls with tiny braids mixed throughout falling down her back, perfectly highlighting the curvature of her waist as she walked away. Even the little gap in her front teeth was sexy to me.

Lara.

Fuck. I know I only spoke to her briefly, but I've never met someone so beautiful, someone who shone so bright. Everything else seems so dull since I left that store. Even my flame, the very magic that grants me eternal life, seems like nothing compared to her. I imagine her as pure light wrapped around me, running through my veins. It's overwhelming. I don't know where these feelings are coming from, but I don't want them to stop.

Lara, my darling Lara.

I rest my head against the wall of the shower and let the water beat against my skin uninterrupted. In my mind, however, I'm still with *her*, with *Lara*, for a few more minutes.

Then I have to face my fiancée.

Chapter Three

Lara

My eyes flick up, scanning the aisles of footwear to make sure no one needs me. I shouldn't have my phone out when I'm at the register, but I'll be damned if I'm gonna stand here for eight hours staring at shoes. Working in a shoe store ain't the most exciting job on the planet, but a job's a job. Discount's nice too.

As I'm scrolling through my apps looking for something to give me a hit of dopamine, I get a notification. *Luke*. I can't help but squeal as I open the text with a quickness.

Luke: Hi, Lara. Injure anyone today?

I wrinkle my nose at his sense of humor. *Dork*.

Me: Hey there, Cutie. That's a way to start a conversation, I guess. But no, not today. How's your tummy? Not too bruised, I hope?

Luke: No lol

Luke: Not bruised.

Me: That's good to know. You won't be too injured to take me out then.

Luke: Guess I won't be. Would you like to? Go out?

Me: I think it was implied that I would, wasn't it?

Luke: I suppose it was. How foolish of me to even ask.

Me: Foolish, Blondie. Clownery, even.

Luke: Hey, what happened to Cutie?

Me: Cute? Are you? I'm starting to forget...I think I need a reminder...

A moment later a notification arrives with a picture attached. A smiling blonde man in a white button-up shirt. *Damn.* He's even more adorable than I remember. I take in every detail of the photo before I reply, and I only stop looking because my cheeks are starting to hurt from how wide I'm smiling.

Me: Yeah, you're pretty alright. I'd be fine with your company.

Luke: High praise!

Luke: How about Friday? Seven? I could pick you up and we could get dinner.

Me: Why don't we meet somewhere instead. Tomorrow, six, early dinner at Eve's Fig downtown?

Luke: I'll see if I can get reservations.

Me: I'll get them squared away. Don't you worry your pretty head.

Luke: Well, alright then. I'll just focus on staying pretty and arriving on time. Let me know if plans change. I can't wait to see you.

Lara: Tomorrow at six.

I know I took control of the whole date thing a little more than I would have in my past relationships, but I wanted to see if it would scare him off. The last guy I dated just wanted a woman he could push around, and he treated me like shit every time I stood up for myself. He was a lying, cheating bastard who made me feel small and weak.

I promised myself never to be with someone like that again. I'm only dating honest sweethearts from now on. Luke seems like a really nice guy so far. Hopefully, I'm getting better at avoiding shady guys than I used to be. I think another broken heart would kill me.

Chapter Four

Luke

"No, Iris, you're already beautiful. You don't need to change anything else. I swear."

I'm exasperated. She's been transforming her appearance little by little for hours now. A freckle here, a half shade lighter hair color there, ever so slightly trimmer around the waist...it's exhausting watching it. She said she wants to make sure she looks perfect, but the fact is I don't care what she looks like. She could be the Venus de Milo and it wouldn't matter.

She even tried to get me to let *her* transform *me* tonight. Fuck that. I told her if I wanted to change, I'd do it myself. All phoenixes have the ability to use our life generation powers to alter material at will, including ourselves. I'm strong enough to alter my looks if I want—to a pretty decent extent. I can even change other people a little, and animals a lot.

Some of us have much stronger abilities than others. Iris, for example, is ridiculously powerful. She's as strong as any Council member, I'd guess. If she wanted to change something about me, I couldn't stop her, and I couldn't do anything to change it back. Thankfully, she just sighs and whines when I don't listen to her and doesn't force me to comply. She's pissed that I won't fix the cowlick in my hair but screw her. I think all the little imperfections are what make people unique and beautiful.

She can get as *flawless* as she wants, but I don't know if she'll ever truly be beautiful to me. She'll always be an obligation, and as much as I want to do right by my people, as much as I never plan on letting Iris feel like I don't care about her, it's exactly that—there's no feelings. All the things that would attract me to someone—kindness, a sense of humor, generosity, uniqueness—are missing from her.

My sister's chihuahua yaps at Iris from the other side of my bedroom door. *Fuck.* Emily knows better than to let her dog out when Iris is here.

"Shut that dog up, Luke," Iris tosses over her shoulder.

"Emily, come get Louie!" I shout as I pick up the poor little guy. She found him wandering in an alley eating garbage a couple years back. He's ugly as sin, smells terrible, and yaps constantly, but he's sweet. Loves to cuddle. "Hurry up!"

"I should go one shade lighter blonde—my brother is going darker blonde this season and I hate twinning with him. My eyelashes could be longer, maybe. What about my ass? Is it too big, do you think?" She turns around in front of the mirror and pouts.

I sigh. It doesn't matter what I say, nothing is ever good enough for her. Still, I have to say something. I turn to her and smile. The dog grunts.

"You know I think you always look great, but of course I'm biased."

Iris curls her lip in disgust at the dog briefly before looking back at the mirror. She tucks her hair behind her ear, pouts her lips at her reflection, then turns back to me. "I know I look great, but how can I look even better?"

Louie growls at Iris. He never growls at anyone else. *Bad choice, doggie.* I have to take this dog out of here before things go south.

"I'll be right back," I say as I attempt to wrestle the now wriggling dog close to my body.

And then, the damn thing bites me. I unfortunately loosen my hold just enough for him to jump to the floor.

"What the hell is that rat doing?" Iris spits out.

I attempt to catch him, but he swoops under the bed. Next thing I know, he's coming around the other side. By the time I stumble around to the other side, he's managed to jump up onto the desk chair and from the desk chair to my desk. The damn thing is usually whining with arthritis and begging to be picked up, but chooses this moment to miraculously heal himself and learn to jump. Great.

"Luke, what the hell? Get him!" Iris snarls.

The chihuahua sniffs the objects on the desk with great interest. I sigh and reach for him. As if in slow motion I watch as Louie does the unthinkable—he pees on Iris's wedding planning notebook.

"Well," Iris says as she takes a deep breath, "I think that's enough of that."

Emily walks in just as Iris lifts the barking dog in one perfectly manicured hand.

"Iris, what are you doing? Give him to me. I'm sorry he got away for a minute. I'll take him back now. Please," Emily begs.

Iris scoffs. "You look like I'm going to kill the disgusting thing. Is that what you think of me? That I'm a murderer?"

Emily shakes her head. "Of course not."

Ah, fuck. This is bad.

"Iris, Emily can take him—"

"I'm only going to make it more enjoyable for everyone. Something pretty. Quiet." Iris smiles as Emily's eyes grow wide in anticipation of whatever awful thing is coming. "I suggest you get a bowl, little sister. Fast."

Louie lets out a sharp cry as he begins to change his shape. Resigned, I lay back against the wall and let out a long breath. This shit is incredibly fucked up, but we're at the point of no return now. Nothing left to do but see what happens, then try to fix it—if we can.

"A big bowl. Lots of water." Iris looks Emily up and down with a mix of curiosity and frustration. "Why are you standing there?"

Emily bolts out of the room and into the kitchen. I can hear water running in the distance as I watch the horror taking place in Iris's hand. By the time Emily gets back, the transformation is complete. Iris is holding on with both hands, laughing as a koi fish flops wildly between them.

"Much better," Iris says as she places the fish gently into the bowl. "You'll have to get an appropriate habitat for it, of course."

Iris smiles as if she's genuinely done Emily a favor—as if this really is a happy ending. I suppose for Iris it is.

The water in the bowl sloshes from Emily's hands shaking, but she says nothing. She stares, white-faced, into the bowl as she turns and exits the room, closing the door behind her. *Fuck.* My poor sister.

"She's not going to talk about it to anyone, I assume?" Iris snaps her neck in my direction and locks eyes with me. There's a definite threat in those eyes, despite her flat expression.

What she did to the dog isn't entirely forbidden in our culture, but it's frowned upon. Transforming without consent is *always* taboo, however, and Iris desperately wants to be on the Council someday. If they have definitive proof that she's going around transforming people's pets without their permission, that's going to be a strike against her for sure. Emily's not so stupid that she'd snitch on Iris and risk getting on her bad side, that I know. *No one* wants to be on Iris's bad side.

"She's not gonna say anything, Iris, believe me."

"Good. Anyway," Iris says as she wipes her palms on my bedspread. "We were talking about my eyelashes."

This continues on for another hour—her making tiny adjustments, while I wonder things like *"How am I going to raise children with someone like this?"* Every time the thought of her taking care of our future kids crosses my mind I feel like I'm going to throw up. Do we really need more people like her in the world? Could I raise them well enough to counteract her influence? The whole thing is giving me a headache. I'm *very* thankful when she finally packs up and gets ready to go.

As I'm happily escorting her to the front door, she turns around and holds up a manicured finger.

"Hold on. Don't forget next weekend we're picking out my shoes."

Ugh. Phoenixes all originally come from Greece, and even though we've been gone for a long time, we still practice the traditions. One is that the groom chooses the bride's wedding shoes. Even tradition cannot escape Iris and her obsessive, controlling ways, so while I may be buying, she's picking them out.

"Of course. See you then."

And then she's out the door.

Iris stayed far too late. And now I need to spend time with my obviously distraught sister to convince her that Iris will fix her dog. Eventually. Probably.

In the past, when she's done fucked up stuff like this, she's fixed it. Even the cat, sort of. Once Iris flexes her power, and makes sure everyone gets her point, it just takes a little begging and adoration to put things to rights. I know what I have to do, especially because Emily is too angry and distraught to deal with Iris. And if it doesn't work...it's a really pretty fish, I guess.

Chapter Five

Luke

I barely get any sleep because of the shit with Iris. It's not difficult to get out of bed, however, as I'm looking forward to my date night with Lara. I haven't been as excited about a date in—well, I've never been this excited about a date. I'm also more than a little anxious considering thoughts of Iris turning Lara into a fish keep running through my mind, but I try to brush those off whenever they pop up.

My day goes painfully slowly because of how much I want it to end. But I leave early and rush home. I shower faster than I've ever showered and dress in the clothes I prepared yesterday. I know I've cut it close on time, but I didn't want to tell her no. She could have said she wanted to meet any time, and I would have found a way to get there.

I pull up to Eve's Fig with one minute to spare. I use the valet parking so that I'm not more than a single minute late. When I get inside, it isn't hard to spot her, considering she's the brightest thing in the restaurant. She's the brightest thing everywhere I've seen her so far.

She's seated already. Her hair is pulled up in a way that lets her high cheekbones shine. The candlelight dances in her dark eyes and it makes me think about having my light inside of her. I almost groan at the thought before pushing it aside. *Not the time for thoughts like that.*

"Lara, I'm so sorry I'm late," I apologize as I take my seat at the table.

"You're one minute late, I think I'll survive. But I appreciate the apology nonetheless." She adjusts the strap of her sundress—the red color of it matches her hair—and smiles.

"Your beneficence will not be forgotten."

We don't have time for further pleasantries before the waiter is upon us. Lara orders red wine, but I get sparkling water. My kind avoids alcohol. Our species enjoys an alcoholic drink called Mastika so much that we can become heavily dependent on it very easily. We're warned away from all alcohol as it can trigger a desire for it in us. Just a weird phoenix thing.

"I have to admit I was pleasantly surprised when you suggested Eve's Fig. It's not easy to find a fellow vegetarian in this part of Texas. Or at least I assume you're one if you're eating here."

Eve's Fig is a strictly vegan restaurant. While people with every diet can and do eat plant-based food, most people don't go out of their way to eat somewhere specifically vegan. Eve's Fig, however, is always busy regardless of its status because of how fantastic the food is.

...Not to mention the high population of animal shifters that live in the area. Most shifters tend to be at least vegetarian, since it's weird for us to eat animals. When your friend might turn into a cow, it's hard to eat beef.

Phoenixes are considered shifters, despite our animal not existing anywhere in the wild. Unicorns and griffins are the same—they don't exist separate from their human half. Griffins eat meat though. A lot of it. And from what the rumors say, it's, uh, not *animal* meat. *Ugh.*

"That I am. I had a feeling you wouldn't be opposed to eating somewhere outside of a steakhouse after seeing the contents of your grocery basket. What were you making, anyway?"

I take a big gulp of my water. Lying isn't fun. Fudging the truth isn't much better. Have to do a lot more of that than I'd like with Lara.

"We just enjoy our food well-spiced in our house. Very well-spiced."

"I get that." She cocks her head. "Who's we?"

"I live with my younger sister. She's currently out of work, so I'm letting her stay with me until she gets a new job. Won't be long."

Not *entirely* a lie. That's why she's staying there now. But I'm supposed to be handing over the house when I marry Iris, as I'm meant to move into hers. It's *much* bigger and we wouldn't need mine any longer. However, if I can somehow get out of this marriage, I won't need to leave and I won't be lying at all. Getting out of a marriage contract that the Council arranged is nearly impossible, however. So, that's a tiny problem. Not going through with the marriage would mean complete isolation from my people, including my family, banishment from the territory of Texas and all other phoenix settlements, and Iris would be able to choose another punishment she saw fit, up to and including a total rebirth. Finding a way out of the contract without those consequences would be nice.

"Well, that's nice of you. I live alone, but my cousin, Vera, comes over to hang out a couple times a week. Speaking of jobs, what kind of work do you do?"

"I'm a dermatologist. I have a clinic in El Paso that just opened recently. And you?"

Lara cringes before taking a drink of her wine. She looks sheepish when she finally answers.

"Well, nothing nearly that exciting. I work retail." She laughs. "I sell overpriced accessories to ladies with too much money."

"Someone has to give them something to do with their money. Better than buying Dalmatian puppies to make coats or whatever else they might do."

"Oh, yes, good point." She nods. "Can't believe I didn't think of it that way."

"Where do you work? Maybe I'll stop by and get some accessories for my sister."

"Oh, lord. You don't want to spend the kind of money those things cost without a discount. But the place I work at is called—"

The waiter interrupts her when he returns to take our order. I'll have to ask her some other time.

We decide to share an order of fried artichoke hearts to start. They're no fun for me to eat due to the lack of spice, but I take a few bites to seem normal. Lara, however, notices my lack of enthusiasm, and slides the bottle of Frank's Red Hot toward me.

"Any good vegetarian restaurant has hot sauce at the ready. There's always at least one in any group that needs everything spicy, I swear." Lara laughs.

"She's not wrong," the waiter laughs as he refills my water.

For our main courses she orders lemongrass tofu tacos, and I get a spicy kimchi BLT (the "B" being tempura tempeh) with a double side of their house extra hot sauce. When the waiter walks away, Lara looks at me with a raised eyebrow.

"What?" I wipe my face to make sure nothing is there.

"You really *do* like it spicy, huh?"

"Oh. That. Yeah. Uh, runs in the family."

"I expected you to make some smarmy comeback about how the dining room isn't the only place you like it spicy or something," she teases.

"Oh, well, sorry. I like it bland in the bedroom. It's like skim milk in there. I just turn off the lights, get in the missionary position, and think of the sexiest woman in history, Margaret Thatcher."

"I almost hope you're not kidding because the Thatcher role play would be something else."

Lara's laugh is infectious. For much of the dinner, my cheeks are sore from how wide I'm smiling. I just can't stop. No one has ever made me feel this way.

"Would you like to see the dessert menu?" the waiter asks when our plates are approaching empty.

I'm full to the brim, can't fathom eating another bite. Then I think of having to end the conversation with Lara for the evening.

And maybe never getting to see her again until I figure things out with Iris. *If* I figure things out.

"Absolutely," I say, "Let's see it."

Chapter Six

Lara

I really like this guy.

"Well, considering the waitstaff has been giving us dirty looks for a while now, I suppose it's time to go," Luke says, "Would you like me to give you a ride home?"

I consider using an app for my own ride. It's the practical thing to do on a first date. But I just don't want my time with Luke to end. Not yet.

"Sure. Thanks. It's not too far."

"That's too bad. I wouldn't mind a long drive. More time with you sounds good." He holds out his arm to help me out of my seat. Goosebumps form on my skin at his touch.

"I suppose I wouldn't mind either."

The ride isn't nearly long enough. Far too much of it is spent with me giving directions or commenting on traffic.

There's no place to park in front of my apartment, so I expect him to stop in the street and wait for me to get out. He doesn't, though.

"Are you gonna kidnap me? Just wanted to give me a last vision of home before driving me to your spooky dungeon?"

"Yep, you caught me." He laughs as he pulls into a parking spot at the far end of my block. "No, there's no dungeon. Just thought I'd walk you to your door, that's all."

"Well, aren't you a gentleman," I say as he comes around the car to help me out.

"It's what Margaret Thatcher would want."

"Oh, lord."

We stop on the stairs, and I take out my keys. Nervously, I wring my hands as we face one another.

"I hope you don't expect to come in. No offense, I just don't let men into my home on the first date."

He smiles sheepishly, pushing back the light hair from his brow.

"I didn't expect it, no. Of course, if you did, I would happily accept, but no, no expectations. I just had to walk you to the door so I could spend every last second possible with you." He chuckles softly, his copper eyes glinting in the yellow light from above the landing. He rubs the back of his neck. *Nervous, ain't ya?*

I admit, I'm nervous too. My heart is racing nearly as fast as my thoughts as I take two steps closer to him. We're nearly pressed together, and slide my hand through his hair where his hand had been just a moment before.

"That doesn't mean I won't be thinking about what would happen if you did join me tonight," I say.

His throat bobs. *There, I've got him.* He'll be thinking of me all night. I internally brush my shoulders off. *Still got it.*

"I, uh, I'll certainly be thinking of you, Lara."

Leaning forward just slightly, raised on the tips of my toes, I wait.

He takes the hint, crosses the distance.

Our kiss is soft, sweet. The hand he lays on my cheek is warm—hot even. His lips are smooth and just as warm. My hands shake as they run along the back of his neck, but only from excitement. He tastes like cinnamon and peppers. There is no clumsiness to our first connection. It's a perfect kiss.

"Lara," he whispers against my lips as we gently pull apart. It sounds like a vow, though he says nothing else.

There's silence between us as we stand, foreheads pressed together, his hands cupping my face. I didn't expect that kiss. I expected a quick goodnight peck, or maybe even some tongue action. What I didn't expect were *feelings*. Something bubbling up from inside telling me *it's him. He's the one.* After *one* kiss!

The way he looks at me makes me hope he's feeling the same thing.

"Luke I–"

"I should go," he says as he suddenly pulls away.

I feel a sense of whiplash at the change in mood. Did I do something wrong?

"See you," he says as he waves.

"Oh, okay. Text me?"

"Of course. Tomorrow. Thank you, Lara."

And then he's walking away, and I'm left standing on the stairs wondering what the hell just happened.

Chapter Seven

Luke

That kiss sealed it.

It wasn't easy getting an appointment with the Council of Phoenixes the same day I called them, but I managed to use a favor the secretary owed me. This can't wait. *Lara* can't wait.

In the old times, the Council would have met in some grand temple with Corinthian columns. Today they meet in a tall office building with big, glass windows. I'm sitting nervously in a gray waiting room for my turn to talk to them. The last time I was here was when they gave me the order to marry Iris. It was not a pleasant day for me. Hopefully, today I'll leave here with better news.

"Mr. Onassis? It's time for your appointment," the secretary announces.

Alright. Here we go. I smooth down the front of my jacket and adjust my tie as I stand. Nothing should be out of place when meeting with these people.

The heavy door thumps solidly behind me as I enter the large space. At the opposite end of the room, four people—three men and one woman—sit behind a desk of highly polished wood. They're all dressed in fine clothes, well-groomed. Each of them gives off an air of power that makes me feel a little sick and *very* weak. Any one of these people could turn me into an ant and crush me with a flick of their finger.

"Take a seat, Mr. Onassis," the woman, Janet Alexopoulou, says. All of them watch as I follow her instructions, sitting in the chair in front of their desk. "What brings you here today?"

"Thank you for seeing me, Ms. Alexopoulou. And, um, everyone. My problem is with my impending marriage. I'd like to request permission to cancel the engagement."

"Your marriage? The one *we* assigned? The one to whom is probably the most desirable, wealthy phoenix woman available?" the man on the far right asks.

The incredulous look on his face tells me it might be harder to convince him to let me out of this than I'd hoped it would be. I slow my breathing and keep my posture straight. I can do this.

"I'm sure you can see many reasons why this would be a less-than-ideal decision, Mr. Onassis," Ms. Alexopoulou replies with a single lifted eyebrow. "And we don't particularly appreciate this gift being rejected, I must admit."

"And I'm sure you're very aware of the consequences of not following through with this contract, should we decide not to change our minds, correct?" the man on the far right asks, the look on his face making it clear he doesn't expect to change his mind.

"Yes, I am *very* aware. I know this was a careful decision by the Council of Phoenixes. Please don't get me wrong, I appreciate the opportunity and I did plan to follow through, I really did. The thing is I've found love. *True Love*. It's new but it's real. I have to follow it, and therefore I must end things with Iris."

Sweat runs down the back of my neck as I watch the four of them exchange glances. Whatever decision they're about to make passes silently between them. They've known one another for hundreds of years. The need to speak passed by long ago.

A third man, Mr. Atlas, sets his elbow on the desk then settles his chin on his hands.

"Mr. Onassis, you know True Love is not taken lightly by our people," Mr. Atlas says. "It is the *only* thing that can break your contract without fault. However, if your feelings are as untried as you are implying, then we would like you to take another week to ensure you are *certain* of them before the contract is broken. Simple infatuation is no excuse to break the contract—it must be *Fated Love* and nothing else. If you are still certain after one week, then you may return and your request will be granted."

It's not exactly what I wanted, but it's better than nothing. I know my feelings for Lara won't change. I felt it in that kiss and the signs have been there since I first saw her. She's my True Love. The Council's answer is as good as a yes. The pressure in my chest relaxes by half.

"Thank you, Mr. Atlas. Thank you, everyone."

"We need you to understand, however," Mr. Atlas interrupts, "Iris is very powerful. Frankly, we don't know how she's going to handle the news. You know how she is, I'm sure. Always had a temper, that one. If she doesn't react well, things could go to shit."

"We are also fully aware that she intends to try for a seat on the Council. She may see this broken contract as bad for her public image. Tread carefully," Ms. Alexopoulou says, long nails tapping on the desk in front of her. "Love and politics don't mix."

I swallow hard at their words. I've never heard a member of the Council speak so bluntly about another phoenix. They're right though. Iris's transformation skills are some of the strongest among the phoenixes. Emily's dog can attest to that. She might be as strong as any of the Council members even. If she does something to me, I won't be able to fight back. I'll be relying on her being a sane person and not reacting to the news with violence. Let's hope that's the case.

"I'm sure everything will be fine. It's True Love, after all." Judging by the somber looks on their faces, the confident smile I attempt does not have the intended reassuring effect.

"You don't know what can happen when a vain, powerful woman is publicly embarrassed," Ms. Alexopoulou replies.

There's a moment of heavy silence before Mr. Atlas slaps a hand on the desk.

"Well, if things go as you expect, we'll see you in a week. If not, then we'll see you at the wedding. Have a good afternoon, Mr. Onassis."

When I exit the building, I lean against the glass for a minute and sigh. *As good as a yes.* I just have to fake it with Iris for a week, make her think everything is okay, and act like everything is normal. Then, I'm free.

Smiling as I walk to my car, absorbing the energizing sun, I text Lara, something I was afraid I may never get to do again. My fingers buzz merrily across the screen as I text her. My True Love.

Me: Hey there. What are you up to today?

I make it to my car and get inside, put on my seatbelt, then feel the buzz of my phone. *Yes!*

Lara: Not much, Blondie. About to go get a coffee. I'm tired. Stayed up too late thinking last night.

Me: Thinking? About what?

Lara: A certain someone.

The grin on my face is so wide it hurts.

Me: Who would that be?

Lara: Well, he's smart, handsome, sweet...

Me: Hmm. He sounds great. I don't know if I have a chance against someone like that.

Lara: Well, maybe he's not that smart.

Me: Then it sounds like I do have a chance. Do you want some company for that coffee?

Lara: If you don't mind seeing me looking like a hot mess.

Me: I don't think it's possible for you to look anything other than beautiful.

Lara: Maybe you are pretty smart after all.

Me: Tell me where to meet you, beautiful.

Chapter Eight

Lara

"Why am I not surprised you're drinking a hot, cinnamon beverage when it's nearly a hundred degrees out? You got a furnace in there or something?" I shake my head at Luke when he walks to the table with his cup of hot cinnamon tea.

"You are what you eat and all that. Can't help that I'm hot stuff." He shrugs and takes a long drink of the boiling hot beverage.

"Oh hell no." I can't help but laugh. The man has the corniest personality. For some reason, I'm a sucker for it. "Anyway, what are you up to today?"

"I have a late shift at the clinic. There is a kid's charity that comes in every month, and we do some free work for them. We keep the clinic open later so we can get as many patients in as possible. After that, I'll probably just grab some food and sleep. How about you?"

"Well, I ain't doing charity work for kids, so whatever I say next will be a let down." We both laugh. "I'll just be working the closing shift. Trying to get those commission sales. Doing the real humanitarian work, saving spotted puppies one sale at a time."

"See, making a difference in the world." He raises his cup. I tap mine to it. "What are you doing tomorrow? It's Saturday. I have it off if you're interested in getting together."

"Well, at least one weekend shift tends to be mandatory in retail. Mine is Sunday this week, so, yeah! If you want to get together tomorrow, I can. I don't know if that's too many days in a row together for you or—"

"Nope, it's perfect," he jumps in. "Did you have a preference for what you'd like to do? Or I could plan something?"

"Hmm. There's this theater near me that plays older films on Saturday evenings. They're playing one this week that's a guilty favorite of mine, but I never got a chance to see it on the big screen when it was first released. It's this video game movie, kind of a spooky one, about this little girl who's sleepwalking and talking about this town. So, her parents take her there to try to figure out what's going on. And—"

He holds his hands up and smiles in a cheeky way that I already know means he's gonna say something goofy.

"Say no more. You want to take me to a spooky movie so that you can pretend to be scared and cling on to my arm. I'll protect you and all of that. You don't have to ask twice."

Yep, goofy.

"Mhm. Sure. Whatever makes you happy, Blondie." I roll my eyes as I take a drink of my iced latte.

"Oof, *Blondie*. That's twice today." He clutches his chest. "I'll have to work hard at the movie tomorrow to earn back my title."

"Wouldn't hurt." I check the time on my phone and see that it's getting uncomfortably close to time for work. "Damn. I got to go. Text me later and I'll give you the details on the theater."

"That I will. You have a wonderful day." He takes hold of my hand as we stand and kisses the back of it. "Until tomorrow."

We part ways, me heading to work a little early so I can toss on some makeup in the office before my shift starts. I don't bother going full glam or anything, but I try to look presentable enough. Our customers can be judgy about that type of thing.

Before I hit the time clock, my phone shakes in my back pocket. I'm not supposed to take it out on the floor, but no one listens to that rule. When there are cute new guys that may text, I certainly ain't gonna follow it. And text he does.

Luke: Are you sure you won't be too scared tomorrow? I don't want you to get nightmares.

Me: Nightmares? Really?

Luke: Yep. You might faint from fright.

Me: Boy, bye.

Luke: Okay, okay. You'll have to make sure to let me know if you need me to stay over and keep you company.

Luke: Because of the nightmares, of course. Just in case.

Me: Uh huh.

Me: You are too goofy. I'm going to work now. See you soon.

Luke: Enjoy your day!

I put away the phone and shake my head. He definitely likes me. No guy texts this much unless they're actually into someone. I'm pretty sure I'm into him too. *Hmm.* Maybe there's a chance he will come over after the movie tomorrow. I won't be having any nightmares, though.

Chapter Nine

Luke

"Perfect seats. Yes!" Lara sits her plump behind down into the cushy red seat in the upper center of the theater. She shoves a handful of salty popcorn into her mouth and chews happily, a rogue piece falling past the cleavage showing in her pale-yellow halter top. "I love movies. Sorry if I get ultra enthusiastic. It's just something I really enjoy, and I don't get to go nearly often enough lately."

"You can be as openly enthusiastic as you want. You being excited makes me feel excited. Seriously." I take a handful of sadly bland popcorn and munch it, barely holding back the huge grin trying to break free.

Her leg shakes with barely contained excitement as she watches the ads play on the big screen. Red licorice snaps loudly as she bites off a chunk of it. Classic candy choice.

"We can go whenever you want," I promise. "I'd be happy to go with you."

"Yeah?" She peels her gaze away from the big screen and locks it to mine. "You like movies, too?"

"Yeah, I like going to the movies." *With you.*

She grins wide. "That's awesome. We should go to the next one of these re-releases. Next week."

"That would be great." Especially since I'll be free from Iris by then. No guilt.

Just then the lights dim and the previews for the next movies start. I love the previews. I'm locked in. We barely talk or interact at all for the entire movie. Turns out, it's now going to be a guilty pleasure of mine, too.

When it's over, we walk outside with the crowd and once we hit the outdoors, we move to the side of the exit. We stand pressed against the brick front of the building where no one is streaming past.

"Alright, you have to admit the guy with the pyramid on his head was kind of hot," Lara says.

I blink at her quietly a few times before responding.

"He was a murderer, Lara."

She shrugs. "Everyone has a few issues."

I rub my forehead as I laugh.

"Okay, what would you like to do now, Mrs. Pyramid Lady?"

"I don't know. I took a cab here. We either walk somewhere or you drive."

"It's kind of casual, but there's a hot dog stand a couple of blocks away."

"Yeah, I know it. But I don't eat meat."

"I know, neither do I. But they have these loaded cheese fries that you can order vegetarian. They're so good. It's a top veggie secret." I must look so proud of myself but it's alright, I feel like peacocking about this incredible find.

"Alright, let's go."

We walk the two short blocks to get the fries, and they're made really quick. They're *so good*. We gobble them up in no time flat, despite the portions being huge.

"What the hell was in these?" She asks through the last mouthful of her fries. "I almost want to eat the container to get more of the taste."

I can feel my eyelids grow heavy as my gaze heats. I think back to my lips on hers.

"That's how I felt after kissing you. Craving your taste. Wanting more and more."

She sets down the fry container and watches me closely.

"Then why did you leave so abruptly? Until you texted me again, I wasn't sure you were even into me. Thought maybe I was a terrible kisser and didn't know it." She huffs out a soft laugh.

"That's definitely not the case." I reach across the table and take her hand in both of mine. "It's just that I felt...I don't know how to say it. It was something *big*. My mind was whirling, and I needed to process it. I'm sorry. The last thing I wanted to do was upset you."

"That's some heavy talk for two and a half dates, Cutie," she says with a nervous, breathy chuckle.

"Well, I'm back to Cutie, so you can't be totally frightened off. Right?" I turn over her hand and massage her palm, my eyes watching the motion to avoid looking into hers. "I'm not too scary, I promise. I'm just a guy who happens to have found someone he really, really likes. A lot. And I don't need to pretend I don't know how I feel just because we haven't known each other very long. I'll save the games for wherever your sexy pyramid headed guy comes from."

I look up and give her the most charming smile I can in my vulnerable state. She's looking at me with her brow furrowed, as if she can't figure out what to make of me. Things are tense between us for a moment until she shakes her head and slaps the table with the hand I'm not holding.

"I told you he was sexy," she says with a laugh. I join her in merriment until we have tears in our eyes, letting the tension of the moment leak out. She sighs. "No, you're not too scary. I don't know though—I still might have nightmares. Might need someone to stay the night and comfort me. Not certain what I should do about that."

"Well, I know a guy who's free tonight. He's nearby. Tall, handsome, doctor. Not afraid of the dark even a little bit."

He's also supposed to go shopping with Iris tomorrow, but we'll ignore that nagging in my gut for the moment. Ugh.

"Sounds perfect. He's gonna need to be able to stay up in bed for a long time. To watch for the nightmares and all. You think he can?" She leans forward, her breasts pressing against the wood picnic table.

"He's got no problem staying up in bed. I can tell you right now you've already kept him up enough."

She smirks as she stands, hikes her purse strap onto her shoulder, and walks back toward the theater. She turns her head toward me over her shoulder and says, "Come on, let's see how long you can stay up."

I stumble rushing out of my seat to go after her, but thankfully manage not to fall. She's turned around and doesn't notice. Good.

My palms are sweating. I can feel the light inside me blazing. She's my *True Love* and she just invited me to spend the night with her. I can't fuck this up.

A girl walks past with a chihuahua. My mind snaps to Iris, fish flopping in her hands as she laughs. My stomach twists for a moment when I look up at Lara, guilt simmering in my guts.

She turns around when she realizes I'm walking behind her at a snail's pace. "You coming or what?"

"Yeah, sorry," I say as I increase my speed, negative thoughts replaced by her glow, "Was just distracted by a fantastic view."

She wiggles her rear end and sticks out her tongue before slapping me on the bicep.

"There's plenty of time to admire the goodies later. Let's get to your car. It's hot as hell out here." She waves a hand in front of her glistening face.

I barely notice the heat. My people come from fire, after all. But if she's overheated and wants to get somewhere cooler, then she's getting what she wants.

"Then let's get you inside. We've got some staying up to do, anyway."

Chapter Ten

Lara

I didn't plan on letting this man into my apartment so soon, but *the best laid plans of mice and men* and all that. Thankfully, I keep the place tidy. I'm also thankful that I shaved and wore damn cute panties. Can never be too prepared.

"I like your apartment. It's very colorful," Luke says as he turns around in the center of my living room, looking at my décor.

It is colorful, he's right. My parents were a little bit of the wannabe hippie type. They loved tie-dye, old Psychedelic poster art, stuff like that. I took after them in that area and my wall art and furnishings definitely show it.

"Let me guess, your house is a lot of beige, right? Maybe some white here and there?" I smirk as I sit on the sofa, draping my arm across the back.

"Hey now!" He drops next to me, mouth open in indignation, "I have a lot of blue in my house. And brown. We have plants too!"

"Plants? My lord, I might faint."

"Lara, are you insinuating I'm boring? Bland?" Luke slaps a hand over his heart.

"I don't think the man who had a basket full of hot peppers when I met him is bland. Are you boring? *Hmm.*" I tap my chin and lean toward him until we're only a few inches apart. "Why don't you show me you know how to have a good time?"

A sudden heat washes over me as Luke leans into my space. Arms on either side of my body, he prowls slowly forward, nose against mine. I'm flat against the sofa and he's looming over me. The heat increases as his breathing grows more rapid. *Is he feverish?* The copper of his eyes seems to almost glow, like coals in a fire. *Maybe I've made a mistake.*

But then he's kissing me, his lips are soft, and it feels like we're breathing from the same lungs. I wrap a leg around his hip, and he moans into the crook of my neck, rubs his clothed erection against the seam of my shorts. He kisses and licks my neck, behind my ear, nips at my earlobe. Our hearts are beating at the same pace.

"Luke. Take me to the bedroom," I whisper.

"Anything, Lara."

I point the way, and he carries me to my room. When he sets me on the bed, I don't stay down—I stand straight up and begin to undress. Luke watches me for a moment before he joins me. His eyes stay on my body as he removes his own clothes, and mine stay on his. I like what I see. A lot. He's fit and has an incredible cock.

The best part is the unexpected tattoos. Loads of fiery feathers all up and down his body. Makes the little goldfish I have on my hip seem like nothing, that's for sure.

"Well, hot damn. Didn't expect that," I say as I finish undressing.

I walk over to him and set my hand against his chest, look up into his eyes. Luke wraps his arms around me and looks at me with a smirk.

"You're exactly what I expected," he says.

"Yeah? What's that?"

"Fucking perfection," he growls as he lifts me, then lays us in the bed.

Everything is a whirl of feelings then as we go from a frantic tangling of tongues, to him licking my neck and chest, to kissing up my thighs. Things begin to come into focus again the first time his tongue touches my clit.

Hot. Fire. Burning.

I pull back from his spicy tongue. *What the fuck was that?* He pulls me back toward him. He softly kisses along my center, relaxing me again. Slowly, he slips a couple fingers inside me, curling just right. Then, as I'm sighing in pleasure, his tongue is back on me.

Spicy!

I start to pull away but he *yoinks* me again.

"Just go with it," he rasps out. "Give it a minute."

"But—"

"Trust me."

Alright, coochie. We're giving this man about ten seconds. If he's still got a jalapeño tongue at that point, we're tapping out!

He restarts from relaxing kisses, then moves on to sigh-inducing inner motions. Once again, he lightly grazes me with his tongue. It's that burning tingle again. I flinch but don't pull away. His tongue makes a second pass, this time lingering a little longer and pressing a little firmer. The burn moves further up my body, like fire creeping up my veins. He kisses, licks, and sucks on my clit for I don't even know how long but in my haze feels like a lifetime.

The burn runs through my entire body. When exactly the feeling turns from unwanted to incredible, I'm unable to place. All I know is that now everything is perfect. *Luke* is perfect. I am a fire only he can feed. He's the oxygen I need to burn.

One more moment and I cry out, my back bowed, hands gripping his pale hair. In the white ceiling, I see visions of flames and feathers before my heart begins to slow down, my blood cools, and the ceiling is nothing more than paint and spackle.

Luke kisses my stomach, my chest, my neck. His hard cock presses into my hip, leaking hot fluid onto my skin. He whispers against my cheek, "Are you alright?"

"I'm more than alright. Confused about what just happened. But very good, thank you," I say, my eyes still on the ceiling. "Did you see the—actually, never mind."

"I'm glad you feel good."

Thankfully, he accepts my odd response without question because I couldn't really explain it if he did question it. Instead, he repositions himself so that he's on all fours, his body caging mine in.

One hand goes to the back of my neck so that he can redirect my attention to him. He kisses me until I'm focused again. When I'm moaning and pushing my hips against him, he pulls his lips away from mine, just until we're far enough apart for him to get words out.

"Shall we then?" he says, barely loud enough for me to hear.

"Yes," I sigh back.

And then we're making love.

Chapter Eleven

Luke

"Yes," she answers me on the slightest of breaths.

A soft shudder of anticipation rolls through me as we arrange our hips, eye contact never breaking. I swallow hard as I line the head of my cock up with the sopping-wet entrance of her cunt. Watching her come on my tongue was nearly enough to have me bursting into flames. I'll certainly have to be careful.

"Oh Luke. Yes." Lara grabs my hips and uses the leverage to push herself forward. My cock enters her several inches in one thrust. "Yes, yes. Fuck."

Very careful. Human woman. Don't start a fire.

It is, in fact, very easy for two phoenixes to start a fire during sex. Even one, when in True Love with a human, can start a fire if they let go of themselves too quickly.

"Slow down, darling," I force out between clenched teeth.

"You don't want to burst yet, huh?" She giggles.

I huff a laugh. *You have no idea.* "Something like that."

Sliding into her achingly slowly, I manage not to set the room ablaze. When I'm fully seated inside her, I take a moment to stop and appreciate the feeling of the two of us, connected. I gaze deeply into her dark brown eyes, wondering how many generations before her had the same eyes—as many as share mine? More? I run my thumb across the wavy baby hair over her forehead, the smooth skin on the flat bridge of her nose, her lips still wet from kisses.

Lara's fingertips dig into my hips as she writhes underneath me. "Come on, lover boy, show me that good time you promised."

"Well," I kiss her as I slowly pull nearly all the way out, "if I promised."

Our next kiss leads to another and another as I glide smoothly in and out of her, gradually building up the light between us. *Don't start a fire*, yes, but the light—that's different.

"Oh fuck, you feel so good," Lara moans. She looks between us, at the point where we connect, and her brow furrows. I distract her with a kiss.

Don't look. I know there's a very soft glow there right now. Barely noticeable. I have to get her mind distracted, so she won't notice it, like I did before with my tongue. I roll us so that we're on our sides, face to face, kissing wildly, while slyly maneuvering myself behind her. Soon enough, she's facing the headboard and I'm entering her beautiful cunt from the back. I stroke her long neck with one hand, keeping her from looking between us, while I circle her clit with the other.

Fuck. It's pat your head and rub your tummy time, for fuck's sake, but I manage to keep my dick inside her, nonetheless.

The light between us begins to shine brighter. It branches off throughout our bodies as it grows into our veins. Lara is now in the place in her mind where she can accept the light, the heat, so I let go of her neck. She whips her body backward, slamming into me with a loud moan. Her cunt is like a vise around my cock as she comes, each pulse squeezing me tighter. The light travels farther up our veins.

When her grip on me softens and her body sags, I let her fall softly to the bed, but I don't stop our session. My desire only increases. Seeing the light through her like marble, feeling my heat in her skin, pushes me nearly to the breaking point. I grab her hips and fuck into her hard, fast.

"Luke, there's a bird," Lara whimpers just before she comes again with a shout.

This time I join her. Releasing inside of her is like nothing I've felt before. It's not about the sex itself—though, of course that's enjoyable—it's the joining of our destiny.

As my seed spills into her soft, warm, insides, I get images of feathers. Soft, white, feathers, and fire. I don't know what it means. Visions are strange and rarely straightforward. But fire must be good for phoenixes. And, of course, Lara and I are fated lovers so whatever else it means could only be positive, I'm sure.

When the light begins to fade, I wrap my arms around Lara and turn her around with me so that we can cuddle face-to-face. She looks bewildered but pleased. I'll have to explain the phoenix thing soon, I suppose.

First, I need to get rid of Iris. One thing at a time.

"That was really—wow," Lara says with a soft laugh.

"A good time?" I smirk.

"Yeah, pretty decent." She smiles.

"Oh, okay. Good to know I have room for improvement."

"You can show me how much you've improved next week, if you like." She raises an eyebrow in question.

"Ah, a second chance. I would like that very much."

"If I didn't have to work tomorrow, I'd be up for giving you chances all night, but—bills don't pay themselves."

"Well, I'll figure out a way to wait. Somehow." I kiss her hand. "We have all the time in the world ahead of us."

Chapter Twelve

Lara

"That'll be five hundred and forty-two dollars, please," I tell the lady at the register. She attempts to tap her card on the machine about seven times before giving up and swiping it. I smile awkwardly when she angrily snatches the receipt from my hand. "Have a fine day now!"

As the aggravated woman nears the exit, the door opens for her. A man's arm holds it as she leaves. Once she's gone, he enters. It's a man I'm beginning to know well. Everything else in the store seems to fade away, leaving only him in my sights. My face lights up with a grin as I dash out from behind the counter and toward the front door.

"Hey there silly goose!" I shout and wrap my arms around Luke as he makes it all the way into the store. I plant a kiss on his cheek with a giggle I know makes me sound like a schoolgirl, but I just can't help. "I missed you as soon as you left this morning, Cutie."

"Silly goose?" a woman's voice asks. "Silly goose? My fiancé Luke? Ah, yes. What a *silly goose* he is."

I feel then how frozen stiff Luke is. When I step away from him, I catch his eyes. All I see in them is shock and sorrow. Behind him is a woman I hadn't seen enter because of how blinded by excitement I was. She's beautiful. And *furious*. There's a smile on her face but it's all *teeth*. Her gold eyes are filled with so much rage they look like they could burst into flames.

I look back at Luke and his face is begging for forgiveness. Copper eyes already half flooded with tears.

I close my expression entirely. No man will ever make me cry in public. Especially not a cheating one. *Fuck that.*

"How do you know my Luke?" the woman asks.

"I don't think I know him at all," I reply, my tone flat, "Clearly, I made a huge mistake."

"Clearly," she replies. "I'm Iris. What's your name?"

She holds out one pale, delicate, hand. My stomach sinks. She looks like a perfect doll. Nothing to be afraid of. But something is *screaming* at me not to touch her.

"You look like you're afraid of me." She laughs, so gentle, like little bells. "You silly goose."

She's right. I'm just being silly.

"I'm Lara. Nice to—" My hand connects with hers and the next thing I know is *pain.*

"Silly, silly goose," the woman, Iris, says in a sing-song voice as she squeezes my hand so hard I feel as if my bones will shatter.

"Iris what are you doing? Stop!" Luke shouts.

My bones *do* shatter then. At least some of them do. Not sure which ones. I can't tell exactly what's happening because *all* of me hurts but I can *hear* the crack of the bones.

"It's not like I'm going to kill her, Luke," Iris says calmly, her voice full of mirth.

"Stop whatever you're doing. She didn't do anything wrong!" Luke says as he grabs her arm.

Iris shoves him off of her with her other hand. He crash-es into a display of heels, knocking everything to the floor. I scream when I see my arm shriveling up in front of me. The sound comes out as a hideous cross between a hiss and a wail.

"Don't stop me, Luke. *You* did this. What were you go-ing to do? Keep a whore on the side during our marriage? Or try to call it off and make me an embarrassment to our people? Ruin my chance at a Council seat? What makes you think you could do that to *me?*" She shrieks out the last word so shrilly I'm surprised our glass displays don't shatter.

My skin itches like it's being pricked with a million pins, and I find myself unable to form words to shout anything at all.

"Iris, please, she's innocent," Luke sobs.

"Just a sweet, innocent thing," Iris says mockingly. She holds me to her chest. "Just a silly little goose."

She's holding me to her chest. My feet can't touch the floor. Oh fuck, oh fuck.

I try my best to get away from her but whatever hold she has on me is as strong as before. The best I can do is wiggle around a lot and flap my arms. My—

I don't have arms. *I don't have arms.*

"Please change her back. I'll never talk to her again. I swear. I'm so sorry," Luke sobs, begging on his knees before Iris.

Wings. I have wings. Not arms.

"You really aren't convincing me. Sort of just seems like you're sorry you got caught," she snaps.

"Please—" he pulls on the hem of her dress.

"I'm tired of you," she says calmly as sets her free hand on Luke's forehead.

His eyes grow wide as he tries to pull away, but it's too late. In a flash of smoke, what was my handsome lover boy is now a majestic copper-colored bird.

The bird is unlike anything I've ever seen. The animal itself stands maybe four feet tall from head to toe, but its tail is at least an additional six feet long. Its feathers are a mix of various shades of orange, red, and yellow, all coated in a metallic copper glaze and tipped in gold. Its eyes are the exact same copper as Luke's. When it opens its mouth to cry mournfully, I see it has a tongue made of flame, real flame. With each cry I see the shaky haze of heat warp its body.

"Oh, quiet," Iris snaps. "I'll turn you back when I'm done. You'll be fine."

The bird—Luke, I suppose—cries out again.

"I said 'quiet!' I'm going home to think. I know very well I'm not *supposed to* transform fellow phoenixes against their will, but I'm sure they'll make an exception considering the circumstances. And like I said, I'll switch you back—eventually. Now, come on. Let's get out of here before someone sees you."

I try to wriggle free from the woman's grasp as we exit the building. She's pushing the Luke-bird along like a slow toddler while we get to her car. I do my best to make it as hard as possible for her to get me inside, but eventually she does, strapping me in with the seatbelt. I manage to make a honking noise during the commotion that, combined with the few physical and verbal clues I have, finally tells me what I am.

A freaking goose. Why couldn't I have called him a silly *lion* or something?

I'm too stunned to think of an escape plan while Iris is shoving a very loud Luke-bird into the trunk. *What will I do now that I'm a goose? Will I be this way forever? Could I be happy like this?* When it slams closed, I'm shocked out of my introspection. My struggling to get free begins anew when Iris gets into the car.

"Alright. Well, that's a no to shoe shopping, I guess. Another day. I'm going to call and see if there's a petting zoo in some shitty little town somewhere that wants a dirty bird," Iris says as she pulls out of the parking lot.

We get right onto the freeway, as it's pretty close to my work. I try to figure out how to get out of the seatbelt with my beak. Or is it my bill? Whatever a goose's mouth is called. Not having any teeth or fingers is a serious issue. I poke at the button from different angles, growing increasingly frustrated. *I will not be in a petting zoo. Argh.*

Suddenly, the back windows roll down and I can feel the wind ruffling my feathers.

"If you can get out of the seatbelt, you're welcome to try your luck through the windows. You'll have a damn hard time finding someone to change you back though, consider that. Who will you go to if you escape? But if you're in my car when we get to my house, I get to do whatever I want with you. I might do something terrible, or I might just change you back and set you free. Haven't decided. Either way, up to you. Go or stay. How about that? Give you a choice?" Iris asks, her eyes flashing like coins in the rear-view mirror. "Not much of one, I admit, but I am feeling generous."

I don't know what the fuck I'll do as a goose out in the wild, but I know I sure as shit don't want whatever happens to me to be left up to that bitch. Finding a fucking wizard or whatever the hell I need to change me back has to got to be the better option. I'll get to Vera and spell out words in the dirt or something. I don't know. I'll figure it out.

I stop my panic struggles and focus on what needs to be done. I just have to push the button, and the seatbelt will come undone. I can do this. It ain't that easy to aim my beak when my eyes are on the side of my head. The monocular vision thing geese have is meant for watching out for predators, not for escaping from luxury vehicles. It just so happens this vehicle is being operated by a maniac.

Ugh, I need to get out. Most of my movement so far has just been panicking, not exactly fine motor skills. But I can learn. I'm smart. I got this.

"You sure that's the best choice? You can stop struggling and relax," says the predator in the rear-view mirror.

Hell no. I try again.

Click.

The seatbelt buckle comes undone. *Yes!* I just barely stop myself from getting tangled in the belt in my hurry to escape. Instead, I wait for it to retract before I scramble to my feet.

Whoa. This feels weird. Big body. Wobbly neck. Skinny legs. Now that there ain't anything holding me down and I have to move on my own, I'm not so sure about this.

"Better get a move on if you want to go, goosey. I'll be home soon," Iris warns.

That's enough to make me sure. I jump onto the door handle and then up to the open window. Okay. Now I need to figure out how to fly. *Boy, the wind sure is moving fast. Pretty wobbly up—*

And then I'm flying. Well, no, I'm not. I'm sort of flapping in the wind in a mostly horizontal but ultimately downward direction. I manage to stay in the air probably about forty seconds, eventually crashing *hard* on the opposite side of the freeway. At least I made it into the grass side of the shoulder and not in the middle of traffic. That's nice. But I hurt my leg pretty bad. My wing too. And my head hurts. *Shit, I don't feel so good.*

"Hey, here's another one. I think that's about it though," a gruff voice says right before someone lifts me off the ground. *Aww damn, not more lifting.*

"Wow, it really got tossed all the way over there? Who knew one little fender bender could have a truck full of geese spread across the highway that far? Wild," an older man says. "Put it in with the others and let's get home before your woman has a shit fit."

"She's gonna already considering all the geese that got hit. You know how she is about profit margins," the younger man says as he opens the back door of a truck. Inside of it are cages and cages of geese. He's about to open one of them when he pauses, looks closely at my face, and steps away from the truck. "Hey, Jim! This goose ain't one of ours."

The man pokes his head out of the driver's side of the truck. "How you know that? Looks like ours."

"We mark ours dumb ass, since they're special and organic or whatever Mazie markets them as. If they aren't marked, she can't do her little marketing videos about them, so they aren't useful to her. Except maybe, I don't know," he looks me over as I try not to pass out from the pain I'm in, "I suppose she could use the feathers. Maybe we could eat it."

"Hell yeah, we could eat it. Get your ass in the truck and let's get back in time to butcher it."

Butcher it. Eat it.

Fucking cheating Luke.

I think at some point women have to wonder if dating is really worth all the trouble.

Chapter Thirteen

Luke

"*LET ME GO YOU FUCKING BITCH!*"

She can't understand me *exactly* when we're in different forms, but Iris gets the point well enough, I'm sure. It'll sound like a cawing bird to anyone else but her and I are both phoenixes—she knows I'm *pissed*.

More than anything though, I'm terrified. I need to get to Lara. When I'm in my bird form, my primal senses are stronger. I can *feel* Lara's essence near me because she's my True Love. We're connected. She probably doesn't believe it at the moment—probably hates me, actually—but it's still true. I can feel her and I know that a moment ago she left the car. I don't know how, seeing as we haven't stopped moving. But she's growing farther and farther away every second.

I have to get to her before she gets hurt. Anything could happen. We're in open country and at the moment she's a fucking farm animal. Some kind of wild animal or huge stray dog could be out there waiting to maul her to death. *Oh fuck.*

"FUCKING LET ME OUT!"

When I shift my position further back I notice something glowing on the trunk door. My heart starts racing. I saw this in a video about how to escape a kidnapping. It's the trunk's emergency release! I never thought I'd actually use this information, but I guess it pays to scroll the Internet's aimless videos for hours in the middle of the night.

Okay. Good. I angle my body so that I can grab it with my talons and beak, making sure I've got a good hold on it, and then *tug.*

POP!

The trunk flies open and my shiny ass is airborne. It's not everyday you see an Ancient Greek phoenix flying above a Texas Highway but for a couple of very confused travelers, today is that day. The Council will not be happy to hear about that, but I think they'll forgive me considering the circumstances.

I get high above the road, making sure to keep in the sunlight so that anyone looking will have to avert their eyes.

I take a deep breath and let myself feel for Lara. Just Lara. *Where are you, my Darling?*

I feel her. She's gotten so far away. But I'm fast. I fly with no regard for secrecy. Fuck trying to hide. No one is paying attention to me anyway. People are dealing with their own bullshit.

It takes a while, but I feel her getting close, really close. I land in a tree outside of a little farm with a sign out front that says "Mazie & Co. Organic, Free Range, All Natural Geese." *What the fuck does that mean? I guess Lara doesn't belong here then, because she's certainly an unnatural goose.* I feel a twinge in my chest that tells me not only is Lara close, but that something's wrong. *Fuck.*

This close to a group of people, I don't want to be too conspicuous. It's one thing to fly around high up above the freeway—people can always assume it was a trick of the light and not an actual shiny, golden bird—but when you're right next to them, things get dicey. That's when they start to freak out. Having to fight for my life would really make it harder to save Lara. So, I'll be careful.

I stick to the shadows as best I can, moving slowly, following the feel of Lara in my chest. The place is nice as far as farms go, I guess. The animals seem like they're taken care of at least. Well, things are nice until I get to the area with the geese. Then it's a shit show.

Two men are letting geese out of crates into a large barn, inspecting them as they're let out. Some of them look all beat up. There's a woman with them yelling and fussing. I can't understand what's going on, so I creep along the side of the truck to get a listen and to better see the geese.

"There better not be a single scratch on any of the last few. I can't believe you. Got ten of my best geese run over," the woman says.

Run over? I almost start to panic before remembering that I can still feel Lara. It wasn't her. If I can feel her, she's alive.

One of the men takes out another crate and dumps two geese out and declares them fine. A final crate comes out, but he doesn't open it right away, his hand pausing on the latch.

"Now, hon, this isn't one of yours. We found this one out wandering. It's a little bit beat up but looks otherwise healthy. I think it might have gotten hit or something. We were thinking if you can't use it for the business we could use it for the home."

"I don't know how I feel about road goose," the woman replies. "Let me see it."

"Sure thing," the man says as he opens the crate and tugs a goose out by the neck.

This one does look a little pitiful. One of its legs is bent wrong and it doesn't look like there's as much strength in its wing as there should be. But the thing most noticeable about it to me is the way it makes my heart race. Even as a goose she's just *brighter* than everything else.

That's my Lara.

Oh no. Oh no no. *That* is Lara. Shit.

The woman looks Lara up and down. She crosses her arms and nods. "That's fine. I can use the feathers. I don't think I can eat roadkill though."

"Hey, it ain't roadkill if it ain't dead!" the second man says with a laugh.

"Whatever you want to call it. Just save me the feathers." She kisses the man holding Lara on the cheek and walks away.

"Alright, Mazie," the man says as he shoves my love back into the crate. He turns to the other man. "Do you happen to know how to cook a goose?"

The men both laugh.

"You know I do! Let's go have a smoke and then get that bird cleaned."

I'm frozen. What is someone even supposed to do in this situation? If I could get to another phoenix, I could ask for help. I don't know if I'd have enough time to get back before...I just need to think of something else.

The men walk toward a different building, one of them carrying the crate. I scurry after, lingering behind a bush in front of the entryway. They talk for just a moment inside but then they're out, stepping around to the side of the building. I take my chance and dart into the open door.

The room inside is as bad as I'd feared. The smell of death permeates the floors. The essence of fear from so many lost lives is so strong I feel like I'm choking on it. In the center of the room sits the crate holding Lara. Above her is a metal funnel of sorts—a killing cone, it's called. I need to get her out of here before she's in that thing. *Oh god. I can't believe this is happening.*

I tap the crate with my beak to get Lara's attention. She raises her head as much as she can in the cramped space to look at me before turning her long neck away. I may not be able to understand her in words but I get the point—she wants nothing to do with me. Rightfully so. I should have been honest. I should have done so many things differently. I wish I could change everything.

I search for the latch on her cage, but when I find it I'm forced to pause. There's no fucking way I can undo that type of latch without hands. At my age I've gotten good with my talons but I'm gonna need something else. *Shit. I could heat up the metal but I'd hurt Lara in the process.*

I look around frantically for anything that could help but nothing comes to mind. I need more time.

Footsteps have my head swinging toward the side of the building. *Okay. I'll just have to wait until they open the cage. Then I'll surprise them. It's my last shot but it'll work. It has to.*

I tuck myself into the corner on top of a barrel, under a shelf, and wait. The two men come in shortly after, laughing about who knows what. One them leans against a table, grinning, as if they aren't planning to murder the love of my life. The other goes right for the cage where they're keeping her. I slowly shuffle forward as he opens the latch. His dry, cracked hand reaches in and pulls out my beloved. She barely fights him. My heart is breaking for her, but my spirit stays strong, as I launch myself from my hiding spot toward the man holding her.

LET GO OF HER!

I snatch at his head with my talons until I see blood. I release a high-pitched screech from the fiery blazes of my throat that I know very well hurts their ears. He drops Lara. As I beat my wings against the man's face, she attempts to stand, but she falls when she puts weight on the broken leg. *Fuck.*

"Goddamnit, get this thing off of me!" the man shouts.

"Yeah, I got it," the other man replies.

Lara flaps her wings but only one works properly. Still, she slowly pushes her way forward. *Come on. Somehow we'll make it out.*

"Hurry it up!" the man shouts as I scratch his face.

Lara looks up at me and for a moment I almost feel as if I hear her. As if she's saying *Goodbye.*

But that can't be right. Romances don't have sad endings. Especially not ours. Especially not when I love her so much. Not when I haven't said I'm sorry. How can—

And then there's a loud, electric buzz against the back of my head and everything goes dark.

.

.

.

.

This is the worst headache I've ever had.

The light slowly returns. My body feels stiff—no, restrained. My thoughts become clearer as I wiggle around, realizing I'm tied up. Then I remember what I'm supposed to be doing.

Lara.

I concentrate until my body is hot enough to burn through the ropes wrapped around me. The cages, I guess, weren't big enough for me. Speaking of cages, I look around the room back to where Lara was and discover that the cage is gone. The scene in the room is entirely different. I feel as if I'm going to be sick.

Below the killing cone is a large cup that contains what can only be one thing—blood. That's how they work. You put the goose in the cone upside down so just their head and neck poke out of the cone. You electrocute them. Slit their throat. Then bleed them out. Clean meat and feathers and they can't make a fuss.

I look to the opposite side of the room and sure enough there are the feathers. *Her* feathers. I look away but see the area where they—well, no one should have to see those parts of the person they love.

I hurry out of the building before I faint. There's no way I want them to capture me. They can't have us both. As soon as I get out of the doorway, I take flight but as I pass by the farmhouse I stall in midair, falling to the ground from pure horror.

I knew they were going to do it but seeing it, really seeing it, is too much.

In front of the setting sun, the two men and the woman are sitting at a wooden table, carving into a roasted goose. The love of my life, my reason for living, served with potatoes.

I stumble away from the gruesome sight, not sure where I'm even going. It doesn't matter anyway. Nothing matters. Life doesn't matter without Lara.

I end up back where I was, facing the building where they butchered her, where her beautiful feathers still lay. I hop up on top of a rusty post that must have been from an old fence. Two of my feathers get snagged on a jagged bit of metal and come free. They float away, heading toward the building. We're supposed to destroy any of our feathers that come loose—leave no proof for humans and all that. But fuck it. I'm not leaving this spot. I'm done.

I'm so sorry, Lara. I wish I could take it back. You deserved so much better.

I'd do anything, be anything, to give you a happily ever after.

Lara, my darling Lara.

Let my last thoughts be of you.

And with that, I start my fire. I will not protect myself from the heat. I will become ash. When my body tries one last time to be reborn from the ashes I will resist and scatter into the wind. This is my death. May I find my way to her so that I may beg for forgiveness.

May I find my way to Lara.

Later

♥

A Department Store, Sometime Later

"Are the feathers in this pillow ethically sourced? Like, were the geese harmed?" the young woman asks the sales associate.

"Uh, yeah, totally ethical," replies the sales associate, who is not trained to work in the bedding department. "Happy geese."

"Well, that's good. I'll buy it then. It's perfect."

The sales associate gladly scans the pillow and watches the woman tap her credit card against the machine to pay. The sooner the woman leaves, the sooner he can go back to his favorite section: footwear.

"Here's your receipt," he says and holds it close to her hand.

The woman recoils as if he was covered in poison.

"I don't need it, thank you," she says before hurrying toward the exit, pausing at the hand sanitizer station on her way.

Some people sure are strange, he thinks as he makes his way to the footwear section. He sighs when sees an orange comforter hanging crookedly off of a display. He feels obligated to adjust it as he passes by.

There, nice and tidy, waiting for just the right customer.

Louie, Etc.

♥

Thank You, Apologies, Justice For the Dog

Thank you to those who took a risk and alpha read my first non-romance story.

I apologize to anyone I made sad. People wanted the backstory, so here it is. I don't know why my brain is the way it is.

I promise the dog will be okay. I'll prove it in the final book in the series!

Texas is for Michaela.

Stuffed Up

♥

by Sylvia Morrow

Content Warnings

♥

Discussions about death, worrying about life after death, gender swap, spicy sex, police encounter, talking about bed bugs, fear of germs, representation of mental illness that includes a character participating in behavior that is harmful to themselves, seeing a cockroach, reckless driving, slight dubcon, outdoor sex, tentacles, tics, implied sex work, chasing, mention of a character from The Phoenix and the Goose burning up, mention of depression at being rejected by a lover.

Chapter One

Anne

Things have changed since Christmas. For one, Ori informed us that the Athans family tree had a hidden branch.

"I can't believe you didn't tell me you had a brother. Of all the secrets to keep!" I shove my glasses up the bridge of my nose, into position. "You know family is important to me!"

"I simply had your best interests at heart, my love." Ori reaches for my hand, an apologetic look in his dark eyes, but I pull away. I'm too upset for hand-holding right now.

"We're not supposed to have secrets. This is really important to me. You broke my trust. You have *family*, Ori! A brother! You might even have other family members out there!" I slap my hands against the sides of my thighs in exasperation. How does he not understand what a big deal this is?

"Well, I do have other family, if you count his partner and daughter. But as for other feathers, I don't think–" Ori doesn't finish that sentence before my eyes nearly bulge out of my head.

"DAUGHTER!?" I shout. "He got someone pregnant? Does that mean I could get pregnant? Oh my God, I'm gonna faint. I'm on birth control, so I'm safe, right? You've never, you know, inside, because of the feathers. So, we're safe, right? But why didn't you tell me it was a possibility?!"

"Oh, calm down." He waves a hand dismissively.

My eyes squint in annoyance at the gesture. He's on thin ice right now.

"Don't tell me to calm down. This is my body. This—"

"She's adopted, darling. You know very well family doesn't have to be about blood. Right, Carl?"

"Uh, yeah. I'd like to stay out of this argument, though. Anne's pretty mad. I'm just gonna work on this map while you two sort this out, if that's alright." Carl turns away from the two of us. I don't blame him. I'd also rather not be having this argument.

Carl has taken up working out the map Ori got from his brother. Carl and I both got copies in our Christmas surprises that we thought were intentionally unlabeled, but it turns out even the original map is incomplete. So, we've had to do all kinds of searches to try to figure out where the heck it's supposed to show. Ori was confident we'd know where the map was supposed to actually be, but he was very wrong. So far, we think it's in South America. Maybe. Carl is trying super hard to figure it out, though.

"*Hmph*. You were barely shocked I kept the *phoenix fire* a secret, a *magic item*, but *this* of all things upsets you? He's only a blanket." Ori crosses his arms, a pout on his perfect lips.

"I could understand why you kept *that* such a big secret, though honestly, I was still kind of mad about it. And by the way, where did you get that? Actually, never mind. We can talk about that later. But you didn't have to keep *Marlon* a secret!" I cross my arms and give him a stern look. "Ori, I want to meet him. AND his family."

"Even the child?" Ori's nose wrinkles in distaste.

"Even the child, Ori."

"Don't blame me when your belongings are sticky." He smooths the front of his jacket, sniffs, and sighs. "I'll need a ride to the store. You know I'd do anything for you, Anne, but if I must do this, I'd prefer not to have to take the bus during rush hour."

Cotton socks slipping a bit on the freshly polished wooden floors, I jog the half room to the door to grab my keys and purse. He may annoy the hell out of me sometimes, but I do always get my way when it's most important. He's stubborn, but he knows when to give up. I'm still mad at him, but for now, I'll let things cool off.

I'm just way too excited about meeting this brother to stay actively angry. *I wonder if he's like Ori? I can't wait to find out.*

"You got it, you grump. We're going to the store, Carl. Need anything?"

"I'm fine. Ooh! We're out of eggs. You wanted to make that cake." He looks at me with his perfect little puppy dog grin. "Oh, and some laundry soap. By the way, I don't know where all my underwear keeps disappearing to, but I'm getting suspicious of the neighbor across the hall. I'm gonna keep an eye on him. No one touches my underwear but us."

I just want to pat him on the head and call him a good boy. In fact, I'll just have to show him what a good boy he is later. Shivers run down my body at the thought of it.

"Anne, you have goosebumps. Are you cold? I'll get you a sweater," Ori says, rubbing his hands up and down my arms.

I slide on my shoes, double-check for hand sanitizer, and take a few calming breaths. *Time to face the world, Anne.*

"Oh, I'm alright, Ori. Everything is alright."

Chapter Two

Ori

Everything is terrible. The store is loud and crowded. One would think that so soon after a gifting holiday, people would be done with their shopping, but it appears they are not. My plan to get in and out quickly dies on the vine the first time we get trapped in an aisle between two carts. I want to confront the rude customers taking their time perusing shampoo, but I can't. If I make a scene, it will only spell trouble.

"Ori, when we get out of this aisle, you go to Marlon, and I'll wait in the car. It'll be faster. This place is nuts today. As excited as I was to meet him, I don't think I can handle it." Anne wraps her arms tightly around herself, and I notice she's looking very pale.

"Alright darling," I say calmingly against her cheek as I embrace her. "Head out and I promise to meet you as soon as I can. I love you. You did wonderfully, by the way. You tried your best."

"Thank you, Ori." She exhales a shuddering breath into my shoulder. "Okay, they finally moved. I'll see you in a bit."

Anne stands on the toes of her sneakers and plants a quick peck on my cheek. I watch as she walks out the door at a brisk pace, rubbing her fingers against one another at her sides the entire way.

"Move, damn it," an old man in a flat cap barks from behind me. There is an entire half of an aisle empty next to us. Why he needs to be directly behind me, I have no clue.

I turn to face him, rage in my eyes. *No one tells me to look away from my Anne.* Nearly reaching for his wrinkled throat, I stop myself. *No,* I need to calm my temper. I retract my hand, straighten my collar, and head toward the bedding aisle. The man grumbles something behind me as I walk away, unaware of how lucky he is.

At first, I don't see Marlon in the bedding area. With a satisfied grin on my face, I turn around, ready to head to the doors.

"Ori? How's it going?" *Marlon.*

"Hello," I reply disappointedly.

"What can I do for you today?" He replies in his bright and sunny way.

"I would like to know if you'd want to—" I take a deep breath and prepare myself for what I know will be an annoying reaction, "—join my family and me for dinner. You could bring your family as well, of course."

"Wow, sure! A family dinner! That's a fantastic idea, Ori!" Marlon says as he *hugs* me.

I cringe as I stand there, arms straight to the side until he gets it out of his system. When he steps away, he's smiling wide, his gapped front teeth on full display.

"Yes. Anyway, Saturday. Seven. If that's alright. Here's my phone number. Text me and I'll give you the address." Reluctantly, I hand him a note with the number on it.

"That sounds fine! We'll be there! Gosh, a family dinner. This is great!"

"Alright, well, goodbye." I walk out quickly to meet my Anne.

"You asked him? He said yes?" Anne asks as soon as I sit in the car and begin to buckle in. The whole car reeks of her pineapple-scented hand sanitizer.

"Unfortunately, yes. Saturday at seven it is."

My phone dings as I receive a text. Normally, I only get texts from Anne or Carl, and Carl only texts if he really needs something. I hope he's alright. When I check my phone, I groan at what I see.

"Marlon," I grumble. "He's already texted. A whole paragraph about how excited he is to see us. Lovely."

I text him our address and nothing else.

"I don't know why you're so opposed to meeting up with him. Everything you've told us about him makes him seem like a nice guy." Anne drives toward our apartment, occasionally shooting the briefest of glances at me out of the side of her eye as we talk.

"He *is* nice. And the *idea* of having a brother is fine. But I don't want anyone else in our family. Just us. I don't want anyone else taking up your time."

"You're afraid I'll be friends with him? Really? Ori, you're ridiculous. I can have friends. You can too. And Carl. Don't be so possessive. *Ugh.*" Anne scrunches her nose in disgust at the word *possessive.* She has no idea what she's just done.

"Anne. I know you like to park on the street but pull into the parking garage today. Park in the darkest spot near the back," I request as we approach home.

"Why? It takes longer to walk from the garage, and it's spooky."

"There'll be something of mine there when we arrive. I need to take it."

"Oh, why are you leaving stuff in the garage? That's weird. Okay. Anyway, here we are." Anne pulls into the spot and turns off the car.

I can hardly get my seatbelt off fast enough, but she takes her time. Her seat is pushed quite far forward because of her height, so there's no way I'm going to be able to take her there. *Damn.*

"Get in the backseat. Now," I command, practically panicking. I didn't think this plan through.

"What?" Anne looks around, checking for some invisible threat. "What's going on?"

"Hurry," I say, scrambling out of my door and into the backseat myself.

Anne quickly follows, confusion on her face. As soon as her door closes, I reach over her shoulder and hit the lock. I tug her body under mine until she's trapped.

"Telling me not to be possessive is quite silly, Anne. From the very start, you've been *mine* and I've been yours." I hold her hair tightly in my fingers, tugging her head back to give me access to her throat. "Have I ever said anything different?"

"No," she whispers.

"Good. You *do* listen. Just to make sure, however, I need to remind you who you belong to." With my free hand, I tug down her leggings and panties, tossing one sneaker into the front seat. When I run my fingers along her center, I find her to be absolutely drenched. "No matter who you're with, where you are, you're *mine*, Anne."

I free my cock from my trousers and with a groan run the head of it along her wet slit. As I'm pressing against her entrance, Anne pushes her hands against my shoulders in a signal to stop. I immediately cease my actions.

"Ori. You forget the other half of that. I'm yours, but you're *mine.*"

Anne lunges forward and meets me in a rough kiss. She wraps her legs around my waist. With as much force as she can in her position, she pushes my shoulders back until I'm in a sitting position with her on top of me. I lift her up to allow her room to pierce herself upon my throbbing cock. We both moan in relief as she sinks slowly down.

"Mine, Ori. Forever." She rides me hard and fast in the back of the vehicle meant for our family.

I look up into her beautiful face as she moans in delight, her mouth partway open, eyes shut, cheeks flushed, and I make a promise.

"Forever."

Chapter Three

Ori

"Ori, stop pacing. You're driving me crazy," Anne says from behind her manhwa.

"I'm not pacing," I reply as I march back and forth in front of the door. *Perhaps I am pacing.*

Carl walks out of the kitchen. As he passes me by, a SMACK sounds, and I jump from the shock of my ass being slapped.

"Carl!" I shout incredulously.

"It's gonna be okay, Ori. No need to be nervous." He smiles.

"I'm not nervous. I just want to get this over with. By the way," I say as a thought comes to me, "you were humming that song earlier, the one you've been humming for days now. The one about the singing map."

Carl shakes his head in confusion.

"I was humming? Wait, the cartoon one—"

"Yes, yes, keep up."

"Oh boy." He rubs his face with the heels of his hands. "The kids at the pool have been singing it and I guess it got stuck. So embarrassing."

"As I was saying, you were humming the song, and I just couldn't help but wonder why the map was given to *Marlon* in particular when I'm the one who wants to use it."

Carl perks back up. "That's a good question, and it's one I've been thinking about, too. What if we need Marlon to figure it out? Maybe even all of us together. The map has a weird feeling to it. I don't know how to explain it. Do you know what I mean?"

"I think I do. Something that makes me want to touch it, almost."

"Yeah, like that. It makes me think that we can't figure it out the normal way. Maybe we can ask him at the dinner party. What do you think?"

"I'm more concerned with what you think."

Carl looks at me as if he's suspicious. *Rude.*

"You want to know what I think? Gosh. How come?"

"The map has been your pet project. It only makes sense you'd have the best idea of how to handle it. Besides, Anne says I have to stop doing everything alone. Or in secret." I brush a piece of lint from my black trousers.

"Oh. Are you going to tell us where you got the flame, then?"

Thankfully, at that moment, there's a knock on the door. I waste no time in getting it open and greeting our guests.

"Come in," I say brusquely.

"Ori, be polite," Anne sighs as she walks over to the group. "Hello, everyone. Welcome to our home. I'm Anne. It's nice to meet you."

I squint as Marlon reaches for Anne's hand. If I see any sign of him draining her life force, there'll be hell to pay.

"Hi there, Anne! I'm Marlon!" He says as he shakes her hand. No draining. Good. "This here is my partner Charlie and our daughter, Imani."

Marlon gestures to the smiling, handsome Black man next to him. I look the man over while he shakes Anne's hand. Anne retains her smile throughout the interaction, though I know she must be working hard to do so. She has been practicing for this, and it's going well so far. I'm proud of her.

Charlie turns to Carl next. They greet each other cheerfully, though I'm not surprised—everyone loves Carl. Charlie looks like a perfectly normal, even above average, man. Well-dressed, good-looking, well-mannered. Why would *he* be with *Marlon*? Strange.

Carl bows to the little girl, who curtsies back to him, the hem of her fluffy white skirt lifting daintily as she giggles. Children especially love Carl, and it appears Imani is no exception. He then turns and offers a princely bow to Anne, who blushes and waves him off with a laugh.

"Marlon, you know Ori. Ori, this is Charlie and Imani," Anne says. When they turn to me and can no longer see her, she points to them and silently mouths the words "*Say hello now!*"

"Hello. I'm glad *you're* the one who got Marlon," I say to Charlie as I shake his hand.

"Thanks," he says with a smile. That smile falters for a moment. "I think so, anyway."

I look down at their child. Her black hair is braided into perfect rows, the ends tied off with white bows. She looks up at me with big brown eyes. We both squint, each assessing the other.

"Hello, child. Please don't make a mess."

"I can't make any promises," she replies in a slightly raspy voice. At least she's honest. "You got any kids? Or pets?"

"No children. And the only pet is Carl, but I don't think he counts."

"Ori! Why would you say that?" Anne gasps.

"What? You think he *does* count as a pet? That would make some of the things we've done highly problematic, Anne."

"He's right, Anne, it would," Carl nods.

"What is my life?" Anne mumbles.

"Speaking of life," I pipe up, happy to find a decent segue. "Marlon, did you ever see that man again? The one who gave you the map?"

"No, I'm sorry Ori," Marlon says with a sad shake of his head. "I really wish I could help you out."

"Well, that's alright, I suppose. We—"

"First, everyone sit down. Let's serve the food before it gets cold. Some of us have digestive systems to tend to," Anne says.

"Oh, fine," I grumble as I wave everyone toward the dinner table.

We all get seated as Carl brings out the food. Those who can eat it *ooh* and *aah* over what a good job he did. Normally, I would be the one doing the cooking, but Carl insisted. He wanted to make a good impression. By the looks on our guests' faces, as the plates are filled, he has. *Good boy.*

I face Marlon, who's seated across from me, and clear my throat to get his attention.

"As I was saying, Carl and I were thinking it over and decided that we need to look at the map *with* you, Marlon. If there's something related to phoenix magic in it, and it was given specifically to you, perhaps you must be the one to unlock its secret." I turn to Carl, who is lifting a forkful of something green from his plate. "Carl, will you retrieve the map, please?"

Carl sets his fork down and scoots his chair back.

"Oh, sure. I'll be right back." Like the wonderfully obedient darling he is, he makes his way to his room.

"Ori, we're in the middle of dinner. Can't you wait?" Anne asks. My far less obedient darling.

"*You* are eating dinner. Marlon and I are not."

She rolls her eyes at my admittedly smug look.

"That's not what I meant. I want to get to know your family before we start on the other stuff."

"Before, after, it doesn't matter." I wave my hand. "Time will matter far less when you're living forever, my love."

Anne sighs and takes a bite of the green stuff just as Carl returns. He slides into his seat and opens the map.

"Here ya go. Oh boy, I'm excited!" he says with one of his charming grins. Everyone at the table smiles back at him. It's impossible not to.

Marlon reaches across the table to take the map Carl hands to him. As both of their hands are still on the map, I remember something I wanted to point out. I take hold of the third corner of it, the final corner that's not torn.

"Oh, before you take it, I wanted to show you that Carl excluded Bolivia earlier today based on—"

The lights overhead flicker rapidly.

"Ori," Marlon says quietly, "something weird's going on with the map."

All three of us still have our hands on it, as if we're afraid to move. In fact, everyone in the room has stilled. There's something strange in the air. An uneasy feeling. I look at the map—there is indeed something happening.

All the ink on the map is running toward the center, while the paper in the torn corner is growing back. We stand in silence as the ink meets to form one black dot. There is a sudden fiery burst from the dot of ink. Veins of fire burn through the paper, drawing a new map. It burns fast and hot and extinguishes as quickly as it is lit. The completed map is much easier to read than the old one.

"Well. It looks like we have our answer." The smile on my face must be a mile wide. *Finally.* "The key to infinite life is in El Paso, Texas."

A sudden chill blows through the room. A deep sense of dread hits like an axe. There's something very *wrong*. Again, the lights flicker.

The child crawls out of her seat and onto my brother's lap. She wraps her arms around his neck and holds him tightly. He looks to be just as relieved to be holding her as she is to be holding him. Anne slides her hand on top of mine and squeezes it.

"Ori, what's happening?" she asks quietly.

"I don't know."

"Daddy, I'm scared," the little girl whispers.

"It's alright, Imani," Charlie assures her. "I think there must be something wrong with the electricity is all. Right, Ori?"

I search the man's deep brown eyes and find encouragement there. I nod.

"Yes. Everyone relax. It's nothing." I smooth my hands down the front of my lapel and adjust the cuffs of my sleeves. "As I was saying, now that we have the location, we plan to extend Anne and Carl's life indefinitely."

The lights go out. Anne and the little girl shriek.

"Anne! Are you okay?" Carl asks, panicking beside me in the dark.

"I'm fine, hold my hand, Carl," she pleads.

"It's alright, honeybee," Marlon soothes the crying child.

Lightning zaps and thunder crashes—*Inside* my apartment.

Out of that lighting, comes a woman—sort of.

There's a glow that lights the dining room enough for us to see the newcomer, and each other, just barely. Where a sensible person would have a head, she has an oversized bird's skull—a crow, perhaps a raven. I'm no bird expert. The rest of her body looks human. She's voluptuous like my Anne, though this *person* is tall, taller than even I. She carries a scythe, which I admit is curious, yes, but mostly terrifying. The white dress she wears is wrapped in garlands of snow-covered pine needles and a matching crown is on her skull. Her very presence radiates a cold that cuts to the very soul.

I don't think I like her very much.

"Ori Athans," she says. Her voice is low and raspy, with a crackle that reminds me of fall leaves underfoot. I swallow hard and sit as straight as I can.

"Hello, yes, that's me. How may I help you?" I reply as quickly as possible. Anne squeezes my hand reassuringly.

"Marlon Sakho," the bird-woman says next.

"What? Me? Oh, boy." Marlon passes a crying Imani to Charlie. "What'd I do?"

"Ori and Marlon, despite my better judgment, since you've awakened, you've been allowed to run about doing whatever you please with life and death. I have, however, received a message that you're planning on acquiring eternal life for humans. I'm here to tell you I've had enough of this nonsense. You are no longer allowed to meddle in Death's affairs. This is your only warning. Any further action of the kind will receive punishment as I see fit, approved in advance by Death himself. Understood?"

"Yes ma'am," replies Marlon immediately.

Pushover. I'll not give up my quest to save my family so easily.

"What gives you the right to come into my home and tell me what to do to protect my family?" Far too upset to sit still, I stand with a slam of my hands against the table.

"Ori, I think maybe you should listen to—" Carl begins, but I don't want to listen.

I see the bird-woman, the supposed employee of *Death*, leaning on her scythe now. She's watching me as if I'm a toddler having a meltdown. It infuriates me even further.

"How dare you try to take away my chance to give everlasting life to my family? I will not comply." I cross my arms and lean against the table to mimic her.

An owl peeks from behind her and looks at me with a *hoot* before going back inside.

"Ori Athans, I *will* prevent that from happening if you insist on trying. You will not like what I have planned."

"You won't change my mind," I reply.

"It's not your mind I'm going to change." She stands straight and holds her scythe in both hands. With a boom that shakes the apartment, she slams the handle into the floor. "Apologies to the rest of you. I know you cared for him, but it had to be done."

With that, there's a sound of fluttering wings, and then she's gone. The lights return to normal, the room temperature is much more comfortable, and the feeling in the air far more pleasant. Anne and Carl are looking down at me with looks of horror on their faces. Both of them have turned white as ghosts. Suddenly, Anne breaks the silence with a near scream of a wail.

My Anne! I attempt to reach for her, but something's wrong—I can't move. Everyone is looking down at me with panic and fear on their faces. Even the child is crying at the sight of me. I want to ask what the hell is going on, but I can't make a sound. In fact, I can't feel my mouth at all.

"Oh Ori, no," Anne sobs as she clutches Carl.

"We'll fix him, Anne. Don't worry." Carl turns to me and smiles with the least believable smile I've ever seen. "We've got you, Ori. It'll be okay."

"But is he okay?" Imani asks her father between sobs.

Anne breaks away from Carl, then reaches for me. Finally, someone can help me figure out what's going on. She plants her face against me and cries, her tears seeping into the fabric of my—hmm. Come to think of it, I'm not sure what part of me she's crying against.

It becomes clear what happened, however, when she wraps her arms around me, holds me to her chest, and carries me to the sofa. My body has changed—a lot. Quite a lot.

In fact, I'm almost certain I'm a pillow.

Chapter Four

Anne

"No, no, bring him back. You have to bring him back. Please help," I beg Marlon. If anyone can help, it has to be him. "Ori saved Carl, right? So, you can save him, maybe."

"I don't know. I can try," he says as he takes a seat next to me.

"Let's hope the psychopomp doesn't come after you for helping him," Charlie says before walking toward the hall with Imani.

"A psycho what?" asks Carl.

"Psychopomp," he says over his shoulder as he pauses. "It's the term for those who work for Death in the physical world. At least, I assume that's what she is. It isn't as if I had time to ask her. Either way, I'd rather not make her mad."

"Understandable. I wish my freaking boyfriend had the same amount of sense, so we wouldn't be in this situation. But no, he always has to be so stubborn." I squeeze pillow-Ori hard as I sob into him. "Is he even in there? Or is it just a regular pillow?"

Marlon sets a hand against the pillow and closes his eyes. His freckled cheeks turn pink as he squeezes his eyes shut and clenches his jaw tightly. After a moment, he relaxes, releasing a long breath. There's a deep frown on his face that is in no way reassuring.

"Well, good news is he's in there. He's not dead, Anne. That's what matters most."

A bit of the tension in my chest loosens. It feels a bit easier to breathe. *He's alive.*

"The bad news, though," Marlon continues, "is that I can't switch him back. Can't even loosen a stitch. He's stuck real good."

My stomach drops. The room feels like it's spinning. *He's stuck.* I don't know what to say. I stare off into the hallway where I can see Imani and Charlie drawing with my Copic markers. *I hope they make sure to put the caps back on,* I think. Why, I don't know—it's not exactly important right now. Maybe I'm going insane.

"Is there anything else we can try? Do you have any ideas? Can he take some of my life or something?" Carl asks Marlon. He puts his arm around me and the warm strength of it brings my focus back to the task at hand.

"I'm as lost as you are. I tried to push some life into him, but nothing happened. But what if—okay, hear me out? What do you think about—and I know this is dangerous, so if it's out of the question I get it—but what if you went to Texas, anyway?" He holds up his hands to stop me when he sees the immediate look of protest on my face. "Not to get eternal life. I'm thinking if Ori and I have transformation abilities, maybe the phoenixes have even stronger or different ones. Maybe they can help bring him back."

I sniffle as I think about it. It's honestly not a bad idea. It might not work out, and it might even get us into trouble, but it's worth a shot. Anything is worth it for him.

"You really think it might work? I need him, Marlon. I love him so much." I can't help but to start crying again. *What am I going to do without him?*

"Well, there's something in Texas that's meant for me, Carl, and Ori. I know that because the map didn't change until all three of us touched it. So, take Ori there and find whatever it is. I have faith in you, Anne. You'll get him back."

"You're not coming with?"

"No, I'm sorry." His shoulders drop with his gaze. He looks at a button on his shirt, twisting it round and round, as he speaks. "I have a family to take care of. A kid. I can't take risks like that. It'd be different if I didn't have Imani. I just worry if something happened to me, that she'd have to go through losing a parent again. I couldn't do that to her."

I lunge for Marlon and give him a big hug, pillow-Ori squished between us. It's not hard to hug Marlon—he's fabric just like Ori, so his touch doesn't bother me much. Plus, he's just kind of a lovable doofus.

"It's okay, Marlon. I understand. Carl and I can take care of it."

"I've always wanted to go on a road trip," Carl says with a grin. "Too bad I can't drive."

"How come? I can teach you some time if you need someone," Marlon says.

"Oh. We're just always worried about my ID. Legal stuff. We got ones good enough to work for day-to-day stuff, but if I get pulled over and they search the system, it's a gamble." Carl scratches the back of his golden neck nervously. He always gets antsy about this stuff.

"You all just need to see Cadillac Dan. He's got the best stuff. The government will think you're fine and dandy in no time." Marlon and Carl exchange smiles that are equally wide and goofy.

"Oh, boy, that's great!" Carl says.

"Oh, I can't wait to call him up," Marlon says.

"Ori," I whisper to my pillow boyfriend, "I think you gave Carl the part of you that was related to Marlon."

A little while later, Marlon, Charlie, and Imani leave with the promise to send Carl information about this Dan guy. It sounds a little sketchy, but Carl is a grown man and allowed to make his own decisions.

"Hey, Anne, do you want anything to eat?" Carl asks on his way to the kitchen.

"No, I'm okay, thanks, sweetie. I'm just gonna take a shower, then go to bed. It's been a tough one." I squeeze Ori with a sigh.

"I get that. You sure you're okay? Do you wanna talk?"

"I'm fine, seriously. Go eat some food. You have a phenomenal figure to maintain, after all." I shake my behind at him on the way into the bedroom.

"Why, thank you!" he shouts. "I will make sure to show you my appreciation for your kind words by offering you a guided tour of my phenomenal figure, free of charge."

I set Ori on the bed and place a kiss on his cotton exterior.

"I love you, Ori. Be right back." I grab my robe off of the back of the door and walk back out into the hall. "Free of charge, Carl? That sounds like a pretty good deal."

"Yep. And it's a private viewing!" he shouts over the clang of pots and pans.

"My goodness! How could I resist?" I laugh as I step into the bathroom. "I'll be out of the shower in a bit."

"Okay, love you, Anne!"

I make the shower as hot as I can stand and undress. Tonight calls for my exfoliating gloves and my antibacterial soap. It's not like I'm fully over my issues with germs, I don't think I'll ever be, but I've improved a lot. These days I really only get worked up when I'm anxious or upset. Tonight, I'm both.

I work the soap into the gloves and begin to scrub myself in the near-scalding water. I'm going to try to act as normal as I can in front of Carl. If we're going to make the long drive to save Ori, we need to remain as calm as possible. I'll need to let these feelings out in private.

Tears run down my face, disappearing with the stream. I scrub myself so hard it hurts. If I can't save Ori, if I fail him, what will I do? How could I forgive myself?

"Hey Anne, are you okay? You've been in there a while," Carl shouts from the other side of the door.

"Yeah, I'm fine. Just got lost in my thoughts," I reply in as cheery a tone as I can muster.

"Oh okay! Just making sure!"

My skin is flaming red when I turn off the water. The lotion stings when I apply it. I don't know how I'll keep pretending I'm alright, but for Carl's sake and most importantly for Ori's sake, I'll keep smiling.

Chapter Five

Carl

It's hard to pretend I'm okay, but for Anne's sake, I've got to.

When Anne comes out of the bathroom, she's smiling, but I can tell she's not okay. Her eyes are bloodshot and the skin on her neck has been scrubbed so red and raw that parts of it even have pinpricks of blood. The parts of her legs peeking out from under her robe are almost as bad. I don't know if I've ever seen her like this. I'm having a hard time deciding if I should acknowledge it. I'm not sure if it would make her feel better or worse. Gosh, this emotional stuff is tough.

"So, uh, you still want to go to bed?" I ask.

"Yeah. We should spend time with Ori."

"He's probably so bored. No phone to scroll on," I huff a soft laugh.

Anne sighs and shakes her head. "I guess I'm happy to have a break from the fake conspiracy videos. His theories about alien politicians were getting old."

"Wait, those were fake?"

Anne blinks at me a few times. "Yes, Carl. We really need to work on you and Ori's media literacy."

We enter the bedroom where Ori is still lying. Not as if he could have gone anywhere else.

Anne hops onto the bed and pulls him to her chest with a tight squeeze. "There's my grumpy guy. I miss you so much already. I'm so sad, honey. I'm so sorry. We're gonna get you back, no matter what."

I pull the blanket back and get into bed next to them. I'll skip my second shower of the day—I can tell Anne needs me now more than I need water time. She leans her head on my shoulder as she gets under the blanket and puts Ori between us.

We sleep with regular Ori between us most of the time. He says he likes to be in the middle to make sure we're both okay. I don't know why he has to make sure we're okay while he's in bed. He doesn't even need to sleep if he doesn't want to. I have a feeling he just likes being snuggled. Not gonna say that to him, though. He'd never admit it.

"Yep, Ori. We have a plan. You're gonna be just fine."

I reach next to me and turn off the light. I can't fall asleep at first, but I fake it pretty well, I think. When I'm positive Anne's asleep—she snores, so it's not hard to tell—I let myself cry a little, quietly. Not gonna let her see it, but I gotta get the tears out. Ori saved my life and if I can't save him, I just don't know what I'll do with myself.

The next day I need to put in vacation time for our road trip. My boss isn't happy about the short notice *at all*, but I tell him it's a family emergency. Thankfully, he signs off on it. I would have had to quit if he hadn't.

Anne picks me up from work so I don't have to take the bus, thank goodness. Her work gave her a lot of trouble about taking time off too, but she got it. Now all we need to do is pack and set our route.

When we're getting out of the car, I get a text from Marlon. I check it out as we're walking to the door. I'm a little confused by it at first—other than what happened to Ori, everything from the dinner party had kind of fled my mind.

Marlon: Heya Carl! Cadillac Dan will be over soon. Hope you'll be home because he doesn't like to be kept waiting. Tried to tell him you might not be there, but he's not very good at replying.

Marlon: Don't look him directly in the eyes. Oh, and don't call him anything other than Cadillac Dan. Not Dan or Cadillac or anything else. And don't argue with him about anything. Actually, don't talk to him unless he talks to you. Seriously.

Marlon: Oh, and I already paid him for you. My apologies for not being able to go on the trip. I'm real sorry about Ori. We love you guys lots.

Marlon: Daddy let me get a fish! I named him Skipper!

Marlon: Sorry, that was Imani.

Wow, Ori was right; he does write long texts.

I tell Anne what the texts say. She frowns and mumbles something about needing a shower before heading to the bedroom. I take that as an okay and text Marlon back.

Me: Okey dokey. Thanks. I hope you got a good-sized tank for the fish.

I'm in the middle of eating a bowl of puffed rice cereal when there's a knock at the door. *Ah, dang.* Anne pokes her head out of the bedroom to watch me answer it. She's still a little wary when it comes to unexpected guests. I open the door and, remembering what Marlon said, lower my eyes when I see a man I don't recognize.

"Are you—"

"Yeah," he replies before I can finish. "Let's get this over with. I got shit to do."

He pulls a roll of blue fabric stuff out of a bag and hammers it into our wall. I'm too nervous to tell him to stop. The way Marlon talked about him makes me feel like I shouldn't get on his bad side.

"Stand there. Straight. Look at the camera."

I do as he says. I don't see his upper face, since it's behind the camera, but I get a better look at him than before. He's younger than I expected. If I had to guess, maybe in his thirties at most. He's thin, kind of short. Medium tan skin tone, dark hair. I'm pretty sure this guy could blend in with seventy percent of the world with no problems and no one would remember him.

Sure would be nice.

He grunts and lowers his camera. I flick my eyes down before he can catch me taking in his appearance.

"You're an unusual-looking motherfucker. Give me some time with this one. Be back about two weeks," he says as he starts tugging nails out of our walls.

"Oh, uh, thanks Cadillac Dan. Do you want my phone number or anything?"

He grunts again as he rolls up the fabric and shoves it into his bag. I'm not sure if that's a no or a yes. When he walks out the door and slams it shut behind him, I assume it's a no.

Anne pokes her head out again and when she sees me locking the door, she flip-flops out in her slippers and robe. She always looks so cute in her pajamas.

"Well, that was weird," she says with a raised eyebrow. She notices the holes in the wall then. "Ugh."

"Yeah, it was." I scratch my head in thought as I feel myself nervously blush. "Hey Anne, am I weird-looking?"

"Huh?" Her eyes snap from the wall to me. "What do you mean?"

"He said I looked unusual. Plus, I know I stand out."

"Yeah, you do. Because you're hot as fuck. You know that. There's the scale thing, but you've been able to pull it off as body art." She puts her hands on the side of my face and looks into my eyes with concern. "What's going on, sweetie? What are you really worried about?"

"Well, we're going on a trip to save Ori. What if someone notices that I'm different and they look too closely into my I.D.? It could mess everything up."

"I'm not going alone, if that's what you're thinking. So, suck it up, buttercup." She pokes my chest. "We're gonna drive safely and be upstanding citizens. It'll be fine. Okay?"

"Okay." I wrap my arms around her waist and kiss the top of her head. "Love you."

"Love you, too. Now, let's pack. We've got a pillow to rescue."

Chapter Six

Ori

Damn it.

They've put me in the backseat.

With all I've been through, you'd think I deserve the passenger seat. At the very least, I could be in someone's lap. Strapped into the backseat all by myself? Really? I can't even see out of the window. The indignity of it all.

We've been driving for hours. How many, I'm not exactly sure. We left at the break of dawn and now it's well past nightfall. Anne said something about looking for a hotel that had a high cleanliness rating on her apps this morning. The GPS has been blabbering about being close for a while now, so we should arrive shortly. Hopefully, they're kind enough not to leave me back here for the night.

"Ugh, I hate hotels," Anne whines.

"I know, you've said it about a million times today," Carl replies.

"But it's just—*ugh.* Sleeping in a public bed and using a public shower? Who knows who touched it last? Or *what* they did! And there could be bugs. *Blood-sucking* bugs that could have bit someone else before biting me, Carl!"

"Yeah, I know Anne. You told me about them." Carl sighs.

"You don't understand, Carl. Being in a hotel is like—it just makes me feel like I'm being touched. Unless I know it's spotless. It has to be spotless."

My poor Anne has been getting progressively more on edge the closer we get to the hotel. She has been doing so well lately with her touch aversion and fear of germs, but this is pushing her limits.

They thought about sleeping in the car but determined it was too risky. If a police officer were to bother them Carl could get in trouble. My poor, darling Anne will be forced to stay at a hotel.

"Turn right at two-point-five miles. Your destination will be on your right," the GPS announces.

They drive quietly the rest of the way, though I'm sure Anne's thoughts are loud and racing. If it were me in Carl's place I'd make sure to say something to distract Anne, even if it was something that annoyed her. *Especially* if it was something that annoyed her—those things distract her from her scary thoughts the best.

"Okay, here we are," she sighs.

"You check in, I'll grab the suitcase."

Anne heads into the lobby while Carl goes to get the suitcase out of the trunk. *Damn it, are they really leaving me out here? Impossible.*

Carl closes the trunk and walks around the car to open the side door. He unbuckles the belt around me and gives me a big squeeze before locking the door behind us.

"Don't worry, Ori, I wouldn't forget you."

Of course, I wasn't worried.

Inside the hotel room, Anne makes sure to set the suitcase inside a plastic bag, on top of the table that's near the door. After checking under the mattress for bed bugs, she pulls her travel blankets out of another plastic bag, lays those on top of the bed, then puts me on top of everything. It seems like a lot of work when, according to my research, there isn't a foolproof way to prevent them. But I know she's worried, so whatever makes her feel safe.

"Are you okay, Anne?" Carl asks.

"Ugh," is all she replies before stepping into the bathroom with her special bar of soap. I can hear her washing her hands. A few moments later, she comes out. "The shower looks okay. We'll just wear flip-flops and avoid touching the curtain, just in case. There are new rolls of toilet paper in here and the toilet looks okay too, I suppose."

"That's good. Now you can relax. You gotta get some sleep. Another long drive tomorrow."

They both get cleaned up and ready for bed while I lay there, uselessly watching some terrible television show; about terrible rich people investing in terrible products. It's surprisingly entertaining and I'm ashamed of myself for enjoying it.

"You know, the last time I had to stay at a hotel, this show was playing," Anne says to Carl as he comes out of the bathroom, drying off his flaxen locks. "I think it must be mandatory for all hotels to play it or something."

"I don't know what it is, but you know I'm not a big T.V. guy." Carl shrugs. He hops onto the bed next to Anne and grins, snatching the remote out of her hand.

"Hey!" she protests as she attempts to snatch it back.

"Nope. This is my first time in a hotel. I'm here with my incredibly gorgeous partner and I think I should have some fun." Carl pats me and nods. "And my other partner too, of course."

Of course. If I had eyes, I'd roll them.

"What kind of fun did you have in mind, Carl? It's kind of weird doing stuff when Ori's like...that." Anne frowns.

"Yeah." Carl frowns in return. After a beat, however, his face lights up. "Well, you used to do stuff when he was a pillow. Why can't you do it again?"

Anne's cheeks turn bright red.

"Well, I mean, I didn't know he was in there."

"He liked it, though. And you know Ori would never in a million years turn you down, Anne."

Damn right.

"I don't know." Anne bites her lip nervously. It makes me want to absolutely ravish her.

With one hand placed on the center of her chest, Carl pushes Anne to the bed. Her hips are lined up with me. All the wonderful things I *could* be doing with them now race through my mind. If I ever get my hands on that bird-woman there'll be hell to pay.

Carl leans over Anne and kisses her softly on the lips, behind the ear, on her neck. He slides his hands into her tank top and pulls her breasts over the top of it. Something about that looks obscene to me and he knows very well how much I love it. Carl is putting on a show for me. *What a good little fishy.*

"Carl, what do you want me to do?" Anne says softly.

She's so easy to convince sometimes. My sweet, moldable, plaything. I love it when she resists, I do, but I love it just as much when she submits.

"Take off your pants, beautiful."

"Okay," she says breathlessly as she slides them off, leaving her little panties on. *Good girl.* "Now what?"

"I want you to show me how you used Ori."

"But it's embarrassing," she whines and looks away.

Carl takes her face in his hands and forces her to look back at him. "Show me, Anne."

Hmm. This dominating side of Carl is new. Not sure what to think of it.

"Okay...okay."

If I had lungs, my breath would stop as Anne straddles me. Carl kneels in front of us and lifts her chin so that she's facing him. He gets close enough to her that their noses nearly touch.

"Watch me as you do it," he says before backing away just a bit.

Anne nods, grabs hold of me and begins to grind against me. It's just like the old days. She's already so very, very wet. It appears she's fond of this dominating Carl. Good to know. I try to make myself as firm as I can without being able to absorb any life force, so that I may best please Anne.

"Good. I like that. Keep fucking Ori for me." Carl grabs hold of Anne's hips and presses her harder against me as she grinds.

"Yes, like that," Anne moans before meeting Carl in a kiss that doesn't stop until she's coming against me.

She breaks away from the kiss to cry out an expletive as Carl continues to move her hips back and forth. When her breathing begins to slow, he pulls her forward, off of me, onto his lap, where they continue kissing, even more passionately than before.

Damn.

"Oh fuck, Carl, that was awesome," Anne laughs against his lips.

"Yeah? You ready for more? Why don't you take those off and I'll hold Ori so he can have a nice view while you ride *me* this time, alright? Let him see that pretty pussy get nice and stuffed, so he knows you're being taken care of."

No one can fill her like I can, but I appreciate the sentiment.

"Yes, yes, I want that," Anne pants as she rushes to slide her panties off.

Anne hands me to Carl, who holds me under one arm, thereby allowing us both an excellent view of the goings-on. Carl hisses in pleasure as Anne slides the tip of his golden cock along her glistening slit. I'm feeling murderous with jealousy, but if anyone is in what's rightfully my place at this moment, I'd rather it be Carl than anyone else.

"That's good Anne. Such a nice, wet cunt. Now fuck me, pretty girl," Carl says as he takes hold of her plump ass, keeping me tucked in tight against him.

I think I'm enjoying this side of Carl. I'll enjoy taming it out of him if he tries it on me. That would be lovely.

Anne sinks onto Carl as they both make delicious sounds. The sight of her impaled on him makes me jealous in the most delightful way. I want to push her farther down upon him and pull her off of him, in equal measure. When he opens his mouth to moan in delight, I can't help but to imagine grabbing him by the hair and forcing my cock into it. Watching those blue eyes look up at me, desperate to please me as he chokes me down? That will never grow old.

I'm going to do the most terrible things to these two when I'm out of this predicament. Such a fantastic time we'll have.

"Carl, I'm gonna come," Anne moans as she fucks herself harder.

"That's it. Just like that," Carl encourages as he rubs her clit with his thumb and guides her with his other hand.

He's gotten good at that. I suppose I haven't been paying attention when it's just the two of them.

Anne comes around him as Carl begins to pant, his stomach muscles flexing beautifully as he pumps up into her. Soon he's coming, pounding hard into her with each thrust, his cum coating his cock in the final pushes. I still find cum fascinating. It's most attractive when it's inside Anne. Especially knowing she won't get pregnant from it, of course. Yet another reason I'm glad we ended up with Carl.

"Thanks, Carl. I needed that," Anne says as she curls up next to me, laying her arms across me and setting her hand on Carl's chest.

"No problemo. I'll be here anytime you need the fish stick!"

"Did you just say *fish stick*?" Anne asks.

Carl just laughs.

"I can't. Goodnight," Anne says as she buries her face against me.

Goodnight, darlings.

Chapter Seven

Anne

There isn't any snow on the ground now, so we're definitely getting closer to El Paso. Which is awesome because I'm sick and tired of driving and staying in hotels. Especially hotels. The second one was not as clean as the first. It wasn't filthy or anything, but there was hair on the sink and a candy wrapper under the bed. If the cleaner missed two things, then who knows what else they skipped?

"Uh, Anne, you're swerving all over again," Carl says, a light panic in his voice.

I snap out of my thoughts of the dirty hotel room and refocus my attention on the road. *Ugh.* My head is all messed up. Worrying about Ori is triggering every ounce of paranoia I have. Earlier today, I even found myself flinching when *Carl* tried to touch me. I've made so much progress and it's all been wiped away. I'm—

"Anne!"

I turn the wheel hard in time to avoid slamming into a road sign. Thank fuck it wasn't another car.

"Hey, maybe we should pull over for a bit or something. That was a really close call, Anne."

"Yeah, maybe."

And then, lights. And sirens.

Of course. It wouldn't be my life if I didn't get tangled up in trouble. It's probably best Ori isn't here to try and save me this time. Taking out a bunch of mall security guards is one thing, but taking out a cop would be a whole other deal.

"Oh no, what are we gonna do? They'll put me in a research facility, and I'll never get out." Carl slaps his hands on his thighs and looks forward, jaw set determinedly. "Alright, I've decided. I'll give myself up without a struggle. That way, they won't search and find Ori. You go on and save him."

I scoff as I put the car in park on the side of the highway. "You will not give yourself up, because nothing is going to happen. We'll figure this out. If they arrest you, don't say anything except that you want a lawyer."

Carl and I both take out our I.D.s and wait for the cop to come to the car. When he finally walks up, I lower my window.

"Hello, officer," I say nervously.

"You want to tell me why you almost hit the sign back there?" he asks. Straight to the point, I guess.

"It's just been a long drive, officer. We're almost at our destination and I suppose I'm getting distracted. I'm sorry."

"And that destination would be where?" he asks.

The cop slowly leans toward my open window so close that his face is just slightly inside. He takes a sharp sniff.

"Uh, El Paso."

He moves maybe an inch further inside and sniffs again.

"You. In the passenger seat. What are you?" he asks, voice alarmingly deeper than before.

Carl startles, looking back and forth before pointing to his chest. "Me? What do you mean, *what* am I?"

"Don't play dumb. What are you?" The cop lowers his sunglasses down the bridge of his nose, revealing widely spaced eyes, yellow but with dark brown circles around the irises.

"I don't know—"

"Fuck it," the cop spits before he grabs me by the neck and tugs me toward his mouth. A mouth that has begun to stretch out into a point filled with really big teeth. Sharp ones. "I'm hungry, kid. As I'm sure you know, there's nothing griffins like more than the fresh meat of sweet girls."

"I did not know that officer," Carl says, his voice shaking. "I don't even know what a griffin is. If you don't eat my girlfriend, I can go get you whatever you want though, I don't mind."

"Just fucking tell me what you are, and you can go. No harm, no foul. I won't even take a single nibble." His teeth drip thick, foul-smelling saliva onto my Hatsune Miku tee. I got it at a concert and can never replace it, but it's going into the trash after this.

"Okay, okay. It's kind of complicated," Carl starts. "I used to just be a regular guy. A human one. And then this man with, uh, yellow eyes came to my work and gave me a map. To Texas. And, uh, I got attacked and I don't know who did it, but they did something weird and it transformed me kind of into a, uh, fish...person? Yeah. And then they ran away. But I saw they also had yellow eyes! So, I thought I should go to Texas and see if someone there could fix me. And that's the truth."

No one would believe that story. *Yikes, Carl.*

After a pause, the cop's grip on my neck loosens slightly. "Yellow like my eyes or different?"

"Uh," Carl pauses here. I know he's thinking of the guy who gave Marlon the map in that bullshit story he just made up, but the problem is Marlon never described that guy's eyes in detail. *Shit.* Carl takes a guess. "Different."

The griffin's hold loosens further. That must've been the right answer. I should have given Carl's storytelling skills more credit.

"And you say you're going to El Paso, huh?"

"Yes, officer."

A long, wheezing breath shoots out of me when the cop lets me go. He steps back from the car, pushes his sunglasses back up his nose, and places his hands on his belt. His mouth—and teeth—smooth back to their original shape. Unfortunately, I still have his nasty, slimy spit on me.

"God damn phoenixes did you dirty, is what it looks like. They're always in someone's business. Those pretentious fuckers are the reason why everyone thinks griffins eat people, you know that?" He shakes his head but then holds out his hands with a smile. "Rumor comes in handy occasionally though, gotta admit. Anyway, you go find 'em and you give 'em hell. They give you any trouble, you call me up and I'll have my cousin pay 'em a visit."

He digs a business card out of his shirt pocket and hands it to me. There's nothing on it but a simple black ink image of a griffin, a phone number, and the name Leonidas.

"Oh, wow," I stutter as I put the card in my wallet.

"Thanks, officer," says Carl.

"Call me Leo," he says as he slaps the roof of our car. "You kids get a move on. El Paso isn't much farther. Don't be running into any signs."

"You got it," I reply as my shaking hand barely manages to fit the key into the ignition. "Thanks again."

As we begin back down the highway toward El Paso, I am quite sure that I will not be running into signs anytime soon. The amount of adrenaline coursing through my veins is going to keep me going for a while.

"Hey, Anne?" Carl turns to me, and I can see from the corner of my eye that his golden scaled skin looks mighty pale right about now.

"Yes, sweetie?"

"I think I liked it better before we knew other stuff existed. Like when we thought me and Ori were the only different kind of people. These griffins and death-bird-ladies and stuff? I don't think I like it." Carl wraps his arms across his chest and leans his head against the window. "I just want things like they used to be. Gosh, I think—and I feel kind of bad saying this because of what happened to him—but I'm mad at Ori."

"Why are you mad at Ori?" I turn to the side quickly to give him a questioning glance. "He's just a pillow. He didn't do anything."

"Not because of anything he did *now*, but before this. I've just been thinking about like how he decided we were gonna do the eternal life thing without asking us. He sassed that bird-woman, that obviously should not have been sassed, which put everyone in danger. He's now at risk of being a pillow forever unless we drive to Texas, a drive that has put me at risk. He didn't tell us anything about where he got the flame, and Marlon didn't know anything about the map, so we've ended up in some sketchy situation, going in totally blind to begin with. If he actually had listened to us and just been rational with the bird-lady or even listened to what we wanted about the life thing from the start, this wouldn't be happening. So, yeah, I'm mad."

Color has returned to Carl's face, only now his cheeks are pretty red. It's clear he's frustrated. It's not easy to make him mad either. But he's got a point. This *is* Ori's fault. And, honestly, Ori has been kind of an ass lately.

"I understand where you're coming from, Carl."

He perks up and turns to me.

"You do? You don't think I'm overreacting?"

"No. Ori needs to really get better about recognizing that this is a three-way relationship, not a dictatorship. I do think the whole growly, protective brat thing is cute on him—whatever the hell that says about me, I don't know—but sometimes I do let him take it too far. It's only healthy to set boundaries. We're in a grown-up relationship and we need to act like grown-ups." I nod my head to mark my final decision.

"Yes! We're going to be so much better about communication. This is great, Anne." He smiles as he watches out the front window. After a moment, he turns to me again. "Hey, since we're being open and stuff, I wanna admit something."

"Oh, no," I mumble. My stomach sinks. *What did I do wrong?*

"You've talked to me about the anime character you said Ori looks like before, well the whole show actually, a whole bunch of times. I mean, a million times. I've always nodded along and pretended like I understood, but the fact is I don't know what you're talking about. Honestly, I don't get most of the references you make. Ori does, because he was just sitting there as a pillow while you watched the shows and played the games and read the mangas, but I wasn't there. When I was a fish, I was in the living room. So, I just pretend like I know because I don't want to feel left out. Sometimes I feel dumb for not knowing normal life stuff already, and I don't want to feel dumb with you guys too." Carl shrugs. The color on his face now is the bright pink of embarrassment.

"Carl, first of all, I've never thought you were dumb. Not knowing something right away just means there's a chance for you to learn. You've done so well with learning to read, cook, do math, you did all that crazy government stuff with Ori—"

"He was so mad when he found out that the grocery delivery people weren't the government 'overlords'," Carl laughs.

"That was funny," I can't help but smile back. "But my point is, you're a smart cookie. You don't have to pretend to know something. I know if you really don't know it, and you want to, you eventually will. You've got tenacity, baby."

I give him a quick wink and get one of his signature handsome, goofy grins in return.

"I am totally making you watch all my shows though. You're not gonna escape, I hope you know that. I don't know how you've missed them so far."

"I think I've been doing other stuff, is all." He shrugs.

"Well, too bad. No more excuses. You, me, and our boyfriend are going to marathon some demonic Victorian butler anime. Then we're gonna get freaky afterwards. Just as soon as we get back from this damned road trip."

Chapter Eight

Ori

They're mad at me. I can't believe it. All I wanted to do was give them eternal life and *they're mad about it.* I'm the one stuck as bedding! This is preposterous.

We've been driving quite a while and all I've been able to do is sit back here and think about the conversation they had earlier. *Mad at me. Hmph!* The GPS says we're nearly to El Paso, which is good because if I have to sit here staring at the back of Carl's seat any longer, I think I'll go insane.

"Your destination is on the left."

Oh good. We're at the motel. Apparently, we're staying here tonight and then in the morning we're going to begin looking for whoever, wherever, or whatever will fix me. We don't have much to go on, so we must have an early start.

"Come on, Ori, let's go," Carl says as he lifts me into his arms. Good thing for him I can't bite him. *Mad at me.*

"Looks like we're supposed to check in out here. Seems kind of, I don't know, shady," Anne says quietly as we approach some sort of fast-food style window. She brings her fist up to knock on the glass. Upon seeing the filth on it, she lowers her hand and looks back at Carl. "Maybe you could. Also, it smells like burnt plastic and acetone over here. Makes my nose feel weird."

"Oh. Huh. That's different." Carl knocks on the glass. Then we wait.

A moment later, a wrinkled face presses against the window. Carl and Anne both jump back in shock before settling.

"Who's that? What do you want? Don't keep cash on the premises. Go on now, git." The person behind the window starts to step away before Carl interrupts.

"I'm sorry, ma'am, we have a reservation."

"A reservation? Here? Doubt it." She looks at Anne. "How many hours you and handsome need?"

"Hours? Uh, all of the night ones, I guess?" Carl replies as he scratches his head, confused.

I, too, am confused. What kind of motel rents by the hour?

"Um, what would you say your cleanliness score is?" Anne asks. Her voice sounds suspiciously shrill. "I thought

I reserved you through my app, but I can't seem to find the reservation all of a sudden. Not sure what's going on."

"Cleanliness score?" The woman opens the window and looks at Anne thoughtfully. "Sugar, I think you made a mistake. As much as I want your money, I'll tell you right now, ain't no way *you* meant to come *here*. I can see that clear as day. Can also tell you with the game and the convention going on at the same time, you ain't gonna find anywhere else to stay tonight. Now, I'll give you the best room I got, but it ain't the Ritz. So, here's some new towels." The lady holds one skeletal hand out past the window. "That'll be sixty dollars."

"Oh." Anne pats her purse in a slow, zombie-like way.

Carl puts his hand over hers to stop her, then reaches for his own wallet. He hands sixty dollars to the woman at the window, then takes the towels and room key from her. Holding me and the suitcase in one arm, Anne's arm and everything else in the other, he escorts us to our room.

Carl adjusts everything in his hold so that he can get the key in position to unlock the door. When he's just about to insert the key, a bug skitters out from inside of the lock. Anne and Carl both jump backwards, Anne screeching in surprise.

"Oh no, Carl, that was a *roach*. I'm done. We're getting in the car."

Anne jogs briskly back toward our vehicle. I don't blame her. The last thing we need is an infestation. Carl sighs and walks after her.

"Well, two out of three motels isn't bad, I guess," Carl mumbles.

I disagree. I believe more than two-thirds of motels should be roach-free. If I had my phone, I would check the statistics. If I were to guess, purely on instinct, I would say at least three-quarters of motels in the country would be roach-free. It would—

"Um, could you move, please?" Anne asks a man leaning against the driver's side door of our car. "This is my car."

Carl moves quickly to reach Anne, stepping in between her and the man.

"It's our car. So, you'll have to move now," he says firmly. *Good work.*

"I'm aware it's yours," the man says, golden-yellow eyes glinting in the moonlight. "That's why I'm here."

What is happening with these yellow eyes? I've never seen them once before this trip and now I've seen two pairs. Plus, there are the ones Marlon told me about. I don't think I'm a fan.

"Okay, well, that's weird, considering we just got here, and we've never met you before. You'll have to excuse me if I don't have time for whatever bullshit scam you're running. I'm tired and want to get in my car. So, move," Anne spits out.

Well, then. Someone found an attitude along the highway. Good girl.

"I promise it's not a scam. I'm only assuming you'd want help with the map now that you're in town. I'm told it doesn't give exact directions." The man crosses his arms and smiles in a cheeky, sideways way that says *got 'em now.*

"The map?" Carl asks, body tense now, voice breathy with interest. "How did you know we have the map?"

"My sister can track the feathers, to an extent. I visited one of you to give you the map. Where is he, anyway? You were both supposed to come."

Feathers? Oh! Right. *Me.*

"Marlon? Oh, he—he had something important to take care of. You don't think I'm one of the feathers, do you? I'm just—" Carl starts, but Anne elbows him gently in the side. She shakes her head *no.*

"I don't think we want to tell you anything, no offense. We don't know you," Anne says.

The man puts his hands in his pockets and shrugs. "None taken. But I really would like you to meet my sister. She's gone to a lot of trouble to get you to El Paso, whoever you are."

Carl and Anne look at each other for a moment, making a silent decision, before Anne turns back to the man. "Alright. What's her address and is she awake? We've got nothing else going on."

"She'll be awake."

He takes a card out of his pocket and holds it out to Anne. Carl takes it from him, then reads the address to her.

"Well, enjoy your evening," the man says as he tips his head to Anne and Carl. "Just, uh, do me a favor. Give her a chance, alright?"

"Huh?" Carl and Anne each look confused.

The man gets into the car next to ours without saying anything else. Anne and Carl wait until he drives away before getting inside.

"That was so weird. Are we really going to go to that address, Carl?" Anne asks.

"I think we have to. We don't have any other clues. What else did we come here for?"

"You're right." Anne blows out a long breath, then puts the address into the phone's GPS and starts the car. "We're doing this for Ori."

Carl looks back at me, in my pathetic position in the backseat, and smiles. "For Ori."

We follow the GPS a bit along the highway. It doesn't take very long to get there, thankfully.

"Wow, okay. This is like a really nice place," Anne says.

"Yeah, gosh. I feel weird that I'm wearing shorts."

"I get that. I'm glad I changed out of the griffin-slobber shirt for more than one reason now, but I still feel underdressed."

What are they going on about?

They exit the vehicle, and Carl comes around the side to fetch me. Immediately upon exiting, I see what the fuss is about. The home is massive. The marble, columns, and lush gardens that are out of place for the climate give the illusion that we're about to step onto the estate of an Ancient Greek deity. It's truly beautiful. But it doesn't inspire a feeling of wonderment in me; in fact, it's quite the opposite.

This place seems frighteningly familiar. I know I've never been here, of course, but I can't help but feel as if I know it. As Anne and Carl walk toward the entrance, I want to scream at them to turn away. Run. There's something inside they should fear. I struggle to do anything I can to warn them, but it's useless. I'm simply a pillow.

Carl rings the bell at the massive wood doors. They're carved with intricate designs of birds and young women frolicking in fountains. They'd be beautiful if I wasn't fearing for the lives of my loved ones.

The door handle turns. With a loud creak, the heavy door opens, revealing a tall, blond woman with golden-yellow eyes to match the man from earlier. With one delicate hand, she gestures inside the building.

Don't go in!

"Hello. Welcome to my home. Please, come in." She shakes her head. "Oh, you must be wondering who I am. So sorry. My name is Iris."

Chapter Nine

Anne

"Um, hello. I'm Anne and this is Carl." Carl takes my hand on the side of his that's not holding Ori and gives it a squeeze. I give him a squeeze back. "Well, let's do this."

We enter the dimly lit building and follow the woman as she makes her way down a long series of halls. She doesn't say much. The whole thing is quiet and awkward. Eventually we end up in a kind of sunroom. It's dark, so moon room now, I suppose. She gestures for us to sit on chairs around a glass table, her to Carl's right and me to his left.

As she settles into her seat, the moon highlights the delicate bones of her face. I can see how incredibly beautiful she must be when there's actually enough light to see her. At the same time, there's something *off* about her. She looks...drained. Yeah, that's it. Kind of like when Ori *takes* from someone, except she doesn't look old, she just looks like she's *missing* something. It's an odd thing to witness and I think if I hadn't seen what Ori could do, I might not have even noticed, might have just thought she looked a little tired or sick. But no, there's something off about her.

"Thank you for coming. I know you came a long way from what my brother told me. I'm sorry I wasn't more upfront with my instructions. Things are a bit tricky when dealing with magical items. Ridiculous rules." She waves a hand as if magical rules are some sort of common annoyance. Maybe for her they are. I'm just going with the flow at this point.

"It's okay. We got here fine. Had some trouble at the start." I shoot a glance at Carl. Not sure when, or if, we should mention Ori. We have to be careful. I suppose we just feel it out. "So, what made you invite us all the way here?"

Her eyes suddenly look as if they're seeing something far, far away. She folds her hands together and clears her throat.

"I need to make amends."

Carl and I glance at each other before he asks, "For what? We've never met."

"No, we haven't. Not really. But there's a part of—" She holds a hand up and looks back and forth between

Carl and me. "I'm sorry, but which of you is the feather? I thought I'd be able to tell, but I guess not."

I reach over the space between our chairs and take Carl's hand. I need to be brave.

"Neither of us. But *the feather* is not doing well. We're here to get him help. If we tell you where he is, do you promise to help him?" My heart races as I wait for an answer. I don't even know if this lady *can* help him, but I need to try.

"Yes, of course," Iris leans forward, and I see sincerity in her eyes. "I swear I'll do whatever I can."

Even though I feel like I'm gonna barf, I give Carl's hand a squeeze and I nod to him. "Alright, Carl. Let's introduce her to Ori."

"So, uh, Iris, this is Ori," Carl lets go of my hand and wraps both arms around the pillow. "He had a little problem with a psycho-something—*psychopomp*, that's what she was. He's stuck as a pillow. If you could turn him back into how he was, that would be great. Thank you."

"Oh." Iris looks at Ori, brow furrowed, for a long moment before looking back to Carl. "Can he hear me? Is he alive?"

"We think so," I reply. "He was a pillow before, when I first met him. It's a long story."

"Has he ever mentioned me? Or anything of life before he was a...pillow?"

"He says he doesn't remember anything clearly, only a few foggy moments. He says that he remembers loving a goose and that the goose got cooked. He also remembers feathers falling off and choosing to die. But that's it. And those memories are all sort of dream-like. He never mentioned you. But you knew him? Really? What was he like?" I tuck my legs under me and get comfortable. *This is fascinating.*

"Well, you must understand first that it wasn't *him*, not really. Your Ori is more akin to his child than anything else. Not even that, exactly. Luke left behind two tiny fragments of infinite life as he chose to take his own. There was a bit of magic in that. It's only happened a few times in all of history. Ori and Marlon are special."

"Luke? That was his—the phoenix's name?" Carl asks.

"Yes. And as to what he was like, well, he was normal. Middle class. Good-looking. He didn't have any particularly unusual habits or interests. An all-around decent fellow, for the most part." She sits back heavily in her seat. "He was my fiancé."

"Considering you don't look like a goose—which is a part of the story that needs explanation, by the way—I'm going to assume there's some drama there." I ask carefully.

"To say the least." Iris sighs. "The *goose* was his True Love. She was a human. He intended to leave me for her. I took it...poorly, and, yes, transformed her into a goose. It was cruel and reckless. Now, I truly did intend to turn her back into a human once I thought they'd both suffered enough, but I was too late. Some farmers found her and ate her. Luke was devastated. You know the rest."

Holy shit. All along, I guess I just kind of thought Ori was actually just a bird or something. Now I find out he came from this horrible tragedy. And that the woman in front of me is responsible for it. *Yikes.*

"So, if you could transform that lady into a goose, then you can fix Ori, right?" Carl asks. *Good job, sweetie, staying on task.*

"There's a slight problem." Iris cringes. "You see, after I discovered what happened, I was, of course, upset. I didn't always have *the best* conscience, but I had one nonetheless. Then when other people found out I was responsible for what happened, I was ostracized. I lost any chance at the position in our people's government that I had dreamed of my entire life. It was awful. Still, I managed. I felt that even though what happened to the woman was terrible, it wasn't my fault that *Luke* chose to die. He could have moved on, eventually. After all, I was never going to be on the Council, and I had to move on. I wasn't going around dying of sadness."

Iris gazes out at the stars while Carl and I exchange confused glances.

"But then, I met Marco." Iris looks back at us. The devastation on her face is unlike anything I've seen before. "He was a unicorn, of all things, that had just moved to El Paso. He was my True Love. His light was brighter than anything else. Seeing him and how pure he was highlighted how sad and dark I had become. He made me want to be better. We had been together for two weeks when we went to the Council to arrange a marriage. Not enough time for gossip to spread to him. When the Council officials went to make the contract, there was a slight snag. My marriage contract with Luke wasn't fully broken. It was fixable, of course—he was well and truly dead. But it did bring up questions about why there were lingering traces of him. Gossamer strands of life still connected to the world. Not so easily ignored, however. It led to Marco asking things about Luke that I'd been avoiding. When he found out what happened, he left me right there in the Council office. Just left. Told me I didn't deserve love. It broke me. I understood Luke then. My heart was being torn to shreds. I truly wanted to die. It was then I promised that no matter what it took, I would find a way to fix something, somehow. The traces from the contract—I'd start there, see what I could find. I found the feathers."

"How does this have to do with why you can't help Ori?" Carl asks, frustration in his voice. *I get it, Carl. This tea is hot, but we've got business.*

"Well, it's how I found you all and brought you here that's the problem. I couldn't find Marlon and Ori. I sought all sorts of magical help, but the most information I got was that there were two feathers. I did, finally, find one vendor who promised me a map that would lead me to the feathers and would, in turn, lead the feathers to me. But he demanded a steep price. Seeing as it was my last resort, I paid it. The price was my flame. And now, here I am, a phoenix with no fire."

She looks at the two of us with her hands upturned like: *and there you have it.* Problem is, I don't have it.

"What does that mean?" Carl asks before I can.

"Oh, I suppose you don't know much about phoenixes. My flame is what gives me my abilities. What lets me live over and over. What lets me transform. I traded mine away. Without it, I can't return Ori to his previous form."

"No, no. We came so far. We were so close." I wrap my arms around my stomach. "What are we supposed to do now? Is there anyone else that can help?"

"No one around here has that type of power. Perhaps a member of the Council, but they may frown upon the feather even existing and demand he be exterminated. Could go either way."

"Oh my god, this can't be happening." *I feel like I'm gonna faint.*

"You said your flame? A phoenix flame?" Carl asks.

"Yes," Iris says.

"Like this?" Carl unzips a pocket on the side of his jean shorts and pulls out the box that Ori presented to us on Christmas. He pops open the lid, revealing the beautiful flame inside. "Ori said it was a phoenix flame."

"You kept it in your *jorts*?" I shout. "Carl!"

"What? I didn't want to just leave it in the car."

"That's it. That's *my* flame," Iris exclaims as she stands up. "How did you get it? I know I didn't trade it to you."

"I don't know, Ori won't tell us," I say. "Does this mean you can help him?"

"Yes," Iris says as she reaches for the box. The light from the flame brings out the gold in her yellow eyes. She looks like a dragon, hungry for treasure. "But if I use it on him, on such a huge task, it will eat up much of the life source. I won't be as strong as I was before afterward."

Carl pulls the box against his chest, out of her reach. "You *will* use it to help him, though?"

Iris blinks, shakes her head, and it's as if a fog has cleared. "Of course. Let me help."

Carl closes his eyes, gives pillow-Ori a kiss, then hands the box to Iris.

Iris inhales the flame in one long breath. Her body gives off a shocking burst of light before settling down to a subtle fading glow. The look she had before, the *drained* look, is gone.

"Alright," she says. "Tell me what he looked like."

Chapter Ten

Ori

"I'm a bit out of practice, so if he doesn't turn out right the first time, you'll have to give me a moment to recharge and I'll fix him," Iris says as she looms over me.

They've got me plopped on the floor, waiting for her to get this over with. I can feel the dirt getting between my fibers. *Terrible.*

"Just try to make him human, I guess," Anne awkwardly laughs.

"I'll try my best." Iris doesn't laugh. *Not reassuring.* "Here we go."

She puts her hands on either side of me. I can feel energy begin to flow throughout my fabric and my feathers. It feels odd, ticklish almost. There's an unexpectedly feminine energy to it, I decide. I wonder if my energy feels masculine. I shall ask Carl. He's been on the end of my transformation.

Hmm. What if he says I have feminine energy? It's possible. I'm not *really* a man, am I? The form I took was only to please my darling. I could be a woman or anything else any day if I wanted to be. How would Anne react? Carl's a good sport. He'd be fine either way. But Anne? Would she still feel the same for me? I wonder...

"Goodness. This one's really stubborn," Iris says. "I've got him started, though. I think I can step away. He's going to go through the whole process now."

I can feel myself stretching. I'm sure I look awful. Carl's face squishes up as he watches me, looking as if he's just been forced to eat maple candy. I suppose that proves me correct.

"Well, that's certainly...something," Iris says, a look of confusion on her face. "I've seen a lot of transformations, but nothing quite like that."

"Don't suppose you've transformed a lot of people made out of fabric, though, have you?" Anne says.

"No, I suppose not."

The process of becoming a person goes much, much faster than the first time. It's not long before I'm in human form. I color myself in with markers Anne sets aside for me from her bag. I make myself a brand-new outfit. I can't see myself, but I'm sure I look fantastic, better than ever.

The others watch in complete silence as I'm perfecting myself, looks of shock on their faces. It could be because of how nice I look. Well, I suppose it's more likely because I'm—

"Ori, why are you a girl?" Carl asks.

"Why not?" I reply, twirling in my pleated black skirt. "Thought I might try something different for a few days."

"Is that—Ori, I have an outfit exactly like that. You can't dress the same as me. It's weird," Anne says.

I huff as I tug at the buttons on the cardigan I copied from Anne. "Fine. I'll try a different style tomorrow. I'm too worn out to change. Now, is that all you're going to say?"

"No, of course not. I'm happy you're back. Obviously I'm shocked though."

"I did try to make him like the pictures you showed me. I don't know what happened." Iris raises her hands defensively, palms in front of her.

"Oh, I was just thinking about what it might be like to be a woman for a bit. It wasn't your doing." I step to Anne, nearly as close as I can get and look down at her. Obviously, I'm still taller than her—I decided to stay the same height as before—because I wouldn't have such a wonderful view of her if I were any shorter. I tuck a lock of hair behind her ear and watch as her cheeks turn red. "I'm certain it'll be fun to experiment. You'll show me how to be a woman, right, darling?"

"Uh-huh. Yep." Anne nods vigorously up at me.

"Wonderful."

A skittering and clinking sound comes from the hallway. I turn to check the floor for some sort of vermin. I want to get rid of it before it scares Anne. Instead of a rat, I find some sort of small, elderly dog entering the room.

"Oh, you'll have to excuse Louie. I'm pet-sitting and he's become needy in his old age," Iris says.

The ugly little dog makes a beeline for Carl and sits at his feet, staring up at him. Carl looks uncomfortably down at the dog and then to Anne.

"Uh, this isn't going to be like the cat café thing, is it?" he asks.

"He seems to like you. Perhaps it's your tattoos. He has a...history with fish." Iris taps on her lap and Louie scurries over to her. "Come on now, you old coot. Leave the guests alone. Took me the last year to get him to trust me, but we've made it."

"Well, thank you for helping me. We'll be going now," I say.

"Ori don't be rude," Anne says. "Thank you so much for your help. It was really interesting getting to know all about the history of the phoenix Ori came from."

"Thank you for letting me help you. I know I'll never be able to change the past, but if there's anything I can do to make things better now, I'll do my best."

"You don't happen to have any sway at any hotels, do you?" Carl asks. "Booking is full everywhere and the place we were going to stay fell through."

"I don't. But I do happen to have a very large home with many bedrooms, each with their own bathroom. If you'd like to stay here tonight, you're more than welcome. I promise Louie and I will not disturb you."

"You know, that would actually be amazing. I'm so exhausted," Anne says.

"Wonderful! Let me lead you up then!" Iris leads the way through the place up to the second floor. "If you get restless, you're welcome to tour the gardens or get a bite in the kitchen. Make yourself at home. Here's your room. Have a lovely night."

The room is, admittedly, fabulous. The bed is bigger than any I've ever seen and incredibly soft. There is a bathtub that could fit a small nation in it in the bathroom. The shower has multiple shower heads. I think Anne nearly dies when she sees that.

"I'll get the suitcase. Be right back," Carl says.

"Let me come with you. I need to stretch my new body a bit," I say. I toss the cardigan on the bed, keeping just the t-shirt underneath. It's too hot here for a sweater. I didn't make myself a bra because Anne says they're horrible. If I'm only going to be a woman for a brief time, then I refuse to subject myself to torture. "There are, of course, a few kinks that need to be worked out."

When we get outside, and I'm no longer terrified, I'm able to take in how truly lovely the place is. It's surrounded by lush gardens, yes, but also trees. The whole place really does feel like a magical oasis.

"Hey, Ori. You want to go for a quick look around?" Carl asks.

"Hmm?" I'm momentarily distracted by inspecting my cleavage. I don't have nearly as much of it as Anne does. I check behind me. Not as much rear, either. I think I look good, though. A willowy silhouette.

"Ori. Walk?" Carl asks again.

"Oh, right. Sure. I'll work out the new legs." We walk toward a forested area. Lovely, fragrant blooms hang from the branches. I hold a leg in front of me and inspect it. "These legs are quite long. Silly things."

"Mhmm," is all Carl replies. Not very talkative tonight, it seems.

"Carl? I don't really know what Anne likes in women. Do you think she'll like me like this?"

"Yep."

How boring.

"Carl," I turn to face him. I hadn't noticed quite how dark and isolated the path we're on has grown until I look at him and realize how difficult it is to make out his features. "You're being very boring."

"Ori," Carl says in an unusually gruff voice. I startle when he puts his hands on my shoulders and turns me around to face away from him.

"What are you doing?" I ask, confused.

"Ori," he says again, this time, however, his mouth is pressed against my neck, his hot breath in my ear. I hear the desperate rumble in his voice when he says one more word:

"Run."

Chapter Eleven

Carl

O ri turns his—her head to look at me. Her jaw is dropped, eyebrows pinched. The look tells me she's appalled at the idea. This'll be fun.

"Fly, little feather, or I'll take you right here where any-one can see."

Her expression turns to shock. She's not used to being spoken to this way, just as I'm not used to acting like this. But my instincts are kicking in—and *fuck,* she looks good like this.

"How dare—*damn it*," Ori says before she takes off running.

I'm so excited I can't help but bounce on the toes of my sneakers as I count down from ten in my head. Her little skirt flaps like fins around her hips as she bounces away from me. *Perfect.* I reach ten as she disappears from sight. Time to go.

I take off in her direction. It doesn't take long before she's in my sight again. I slow down so that she doesn't see me—I want this to last a little bit longer. She tugs the hem of her white t-shirt off of a low branch with a frustrated growl. The hardness of her nipples is visible in her shirt. I wonder why she didn't make herself a bra. Huh.

"Fucking fish," Ori mumbles, barely loud enough for me to hear as I approach.

She's gone further into the trees. Low branches are scraping my shins and I'm currently regretting wearing shorts. *'Jorts',* according to Anne. I'll wait until Ori gets into some kind of clearing before I pounce.

For a second, I lose track of her. I listen for her but find a visible clue first—a feather. She must have gotten snagged on a bush or something. *Poor little pillow.*

And there she is. Running across a grassy area between the trees. The moonlight reflects blue on Ori's shoulder-length black hair. The shadows bring out the sharp proportions of her face. And I can see them well when she turns and sees me coming closer to her.

"Oh, hell. Carl, you better—"

And then I'm on her. I wrap my arms around her and drag her to the grass. Ori struggles against me, cursing at me, nipping at my hands. But I know it's not serious. I know she wants this as much as I do. Because if Ori wanted to hurt me, she could. If Ori wanted me to stop, she'd tell me.

"If you really want me to stop, you know the safe word," I say softly. It's better to be sure.

"That safe word is for you, not me. I don't need safe words. What do you think I am?" Ori snaps back.

I push Ori flat to the ground and twist her head to the side. I grind my hips into her ass as I growl into her ear, "I think you're a slutty little pillow who's gonna take my cock in about thirty seconds. If you have a problem with that, you say the safe word. Got it?"

I sit up on my knees and look down at her, indecision on her face as I push her skirt up. Her little white panties don't slide off her ass as smoothly as they do Anne's—the fabrics catch on each other just a little—but I do drag them down all the way off of her long, pale legs. I toss them behind me.

"Oh, damn it, Carl," Ori whines as she attempts to push herself up, "This is so embarrassing."

I push her back down, lift her ass. "I said, got it?"

"Yes," Ori answers quietly, reluctantly.

I unzip my shorts as I stare at Ori's gorgeous cunt. Whatever magic she took from that lady, she really used it well. I tug my shorts and underwear down, letting my cock spring out. The first touch of my tip against her slit makes her jerk away from me, but I pull her back.

"Really?" she whines.

"You can take it, Ori."

"Of course I can," she replies, that signature Ori cockiness showing itself.

"Oh yeah?" *Might as well take advantage of her little attitude.* "You sure about that? I mean, I know Anne sure likes it, but—"

She squints at me. "Fuck me, Carl. And you better do it right. I'm not wasting my time out here."

I grin as I line myself up with her entrance. *God, I love that attitude.* "You got it."

I drive into Ori with one hard thrust. She loses her position propped on her elbows, falling face-first to the ground. Ori spits out grass as she lifts her head again.

"Is that it?" she taunts. "Are you just going to stay stuffed in there forever?"

I can't help but laugh and shake my head as I begin to push in and out of her insides. She's fabric inside, but it's smooth. There's a squeezing, rippling going along with each of my thrusts, acting almost like a strange sort of machine pushing and pulling me inside, keeping me from getting friction burn. *A conveyor belt of cunt.* The thought makes me laugh harder.

"What are you laughing at?" Ori snaps.

"Not at you. You're perfect. I love what you're doing for me inside. Feels so good," I rasp as I pump faster into her.

"I'm not doing anything. Don't know what you mean," she mumbles. *Sure.*

I slip my hand around her narrow hips to find her swollen clit. As soon as I touch it, Ori moans in a ridiculously delicious way.

"So that's what that feels like," she says, moaning again, as I rub her in brisk circles. "I see why Anne likes it."

"Yeah? Anne loves it when I fuck her Ori. When you're working, we head to the second bedroom, and I fill her with so much cum it drips down her legs when she gets out of bed."

"Carl, you know you can't please her like I can. No one can."

I press her clit firmer as I circle it. Ori drives her fingers into the grass with a clench and a groan.

"She loves it, Ori. Now you know why." I slam into her over and over as her body begins to tense. "Look at that pretty little pillow, stuffed so full."

Ori cries out, her back bowing, head thrown back. "Fuck, yes. Yes!"

The sight is fan-fucking-tastic. Though, I have to wonder if I'll ever take Ori when she's in her regular form. I bet he'd be just as beautiful. Thinking of Ori's other body and what we've done puts a mischievous thought into my head. I put my mouth next to her ear so there's no way she can miss what I'm about to say.

"Ready for my cum, *little omega*?"

An elbow jabs into my side, before I'm tossed flat onto my back with an *oof*. Crouched over me is a ticked-off looking pillow-lady.

"Something I said?" I say with a chuckle.

"I am *not* the omega," she grinds out between clenched teeth. Ori aligns her center with my hard cock and slowly begins to sink onto it. I cup her firm ass in my palms, but she pulls them away, slamming my hands to the ground. "And you'll come when I want you to."

Ori starts a smooth, rhythmic grinding that has me at the edge in no time. Just when I think I'm gonna come, Ori reveals another semi-creepy trick by unfurling short tentacles inside her. She pauses her movements while her internal tentacles squeeze near the head of my dick. Once the immediate urge to come passes, she releases me and continues her motions.

We go on like this a couple more times until finally Ori releases my hands, allowing me to stroke her soft fabric. She rides me faster, both of us moaning now. Ori then clenches around me, coming hard. I groan as I'm at last able to release inside of her. I'm breathing hard as I come down, staring up at the moon. *What a night.*

"Well. That's that then," Ori says as she climbs off of me. "Time for underwear."

I look down only to see a wet mess of little, downy feathers on and around my softening cock. *Huh.* I guess she still comes feathers.

"How romantic of you," I laugh.

"There'll be plenty of time for romance. Right now, we need to get back inside before Anne starts to panic."

Chapter Twelve

Anne

I *never want to leave this shower.*

It's so fancy. I'm sprayed from several directions at once. She has individually packaged guest soaps, and they smell *so good*. The shampoo and conditioner are the type I will never be able to afford. I am going to smell like a tea tree by the time I get out of here, and I'm perfectly okay with that.

"Anne! Don't worry, we're okay!" Carl shouts from behind the shower door. "I'm sorry it took so long!"

"Yes, please forgive us for the delay, darling," Ori adds.

How long have I been in here? I didn't even realize they'd apparently been gone a long time.

"Oh, uh, it's fine. I totally knew you guys were taking a long time, but, uh, I knew you'd be fine."

"Carl, she didn't even realize we'd been gone!"

"Ori, that's not true. I knew you were gone, I just didn't know I had been in here a long time. This thing is freaking marvelous."

A few seconds later, the door opens and a nude Carl joins me in the spray. *We really just don't have enough boundaries.*

"Wow, this is great!" Carl says as he inspects the various shower heads.

I notice a swirl of feathers getting caught by the drain's hair catcher. My eyes drag up Carl's legs and open wide when I see all the little feathers stuck to his groin.

"So, what did you two do while you were out?" I ask Carl with a raised eyebrow.

"Nothing!" Ori shouts.

"I had sex with Ori. We used her new vagina," Carl says with a grin. "She still comes feathers."

I have to cover my mouth to keep my laugh in. What happened isn't funny—I'm sure it was romantic and beautiful and whatnot—it's just the way he said it. If I laugh, Ori will think I'm making fun of her.

"Carl!" Ori says, tone indignant, "I'm sure Anne doesn't want to hear about that."

"On the contrary, I'm pretty sure I want to know everything."

"Well, first Ori and I went on a walk. Then—" Carl starts before the shower door opens.

"I'm sure she's only being polite," she grouses. "Please hurry up, we have driving to do in the morning."

"Okay, grumpy," I say as I close the door. I raise my face to feel the perfect water pressure again. "One more rinse and I'm out."

When my hair is dry and we're all cuddled together in the bed, I wrap my arms around Ori and give her a kiss on the cheek.

"I love you. I'm so happy you're back," I say into her neck as I snuggle her tight.

"Yes, well, you know I'll always find my way to you. And I had full faith that you would bring me back. The three of us are inseparable, darling."

"Absolutely," Carl says as wraps his arm around Ori's waist. "Isn't it great?"

We sleep for not nearly long enough, but have to get up as early as we can. I'm getting *really* homesick and I'm going to drive as long as possible between stops. We only want to spend two nights at hotels max. No way am I doing three stays on the way back.

"How was your sleep?" Iris asks as she enters the kitchen.

She looks better than she did when we got here. There's more life to her now. She opens the fridge and takes out a bowl of jalapeños.

"We slept really well. Thank you again," I say.

Iris sets the jalapeños on the counter and sprinkles them with a heavy dose of cinnamon, balsamic vinegar, and cayenne pepper. She stabs one of the peppers with a fork and takes a bite. Carl and I exchange confused glances, while Ori taps her chin.

"Is that something people like? I cook for Anne and Carl but would never think of that," Ori says.

"Uh, I think we will pass. No offense, Iris." I cringe.

"None taken. Phoenixes just have a bit of an odd diet."

"Ah, that makes sense," Ori says. Then, suddenly, one of Ori's legs gives out, flattening like it did the first day I met her. She looks up at me with panic as she wobbles on one foot. "I thought this was over with."

"What's going on?" Iris asks.

I explain to her about how when I first met Ori he needed to drain life force from people or else he'd get all floppy, and how when Ori killed those security guards he didn't have to do it anymore.

"I can't very well take life anymore though," Ori says. "After that bird-woman came after me and told me not to mess with life, and turned me back into a pillow when

I protested, I think it's safe to say I'm no longer able to intentionally shorten people's life spans without consequence."

"Well, what are we gonna do then? We can't just let you get all flat," Carl says as he holds Ori up by the waist.

"Wait, that's how you were regenerating your powers?" Iris asks, confusion clear on her face. "You know you don't need to do that."

"What do you mean?" Ori asks.

"You just need to spend more time in the sun, Ori. That's how phoenixes replenish our abilities. Yes, we could drain life force, but we wouldn't dare."

"I spend plenty of time in the sun," Ori pouts.

I think about how he spent his beginning in my bedroom, then he was forced to stay indoors for a while, then he got an indoor job, how all his hobbies are indoors...

"Well, not really," I shrug. "We could all probably get out of the house more."

"There. You sit in the front seat of your drive and soak up the sunshine. You'll be back to normal in no time," Iris says as she bites into another pepper.

"Of course, I'll sit in the front," Ori scoffs. *Oh, Ori.* The scowl on her face relaxes as she leans closer to Iris. "I don't suppose you have any other tips and tricks I may want to know, do you?"

"Hmm. Not really sure. I could call you if I think of anything, perhaps?"

Ori returns to her grumpy posture. "How about text?"

"That's fine," Iris laughs. "I'm old and still used to calling."

"You can't be that old," I say. She looks like she's in her late twenties at most.

"Well, I'm not old for a phoenix, but compared to a human I am. I'll be three hundred and fifty soon enough. We do live very long lives." Her eyes turn dull for a brief moment. "Unless we end them by intentional fire, of course."

"How will my life end? I can't set myself on fire. Well, I could, and my fabric would burn, but you're saying for the feather it must be a phoenix flame, correct?" Ori asks.

My stomach gurgles at the thought of Ori dying. I don't know why he would even want to know this. When I look at Carl, I can see his jaw is clenched, and I know he doesn't like the thought either. A familiar anxiety washes over me and I find myself rubbing my fingertips together. *Damn it.*

"Correct. Who knows, though, you could be different. You're not *really* a phoenix, so the normal rules are out the window, aren't they?" Iris shrugs as she bites into another pepper.

"Let's not think about that right now. We just got you back. You can text if you want to talk about it later," I say.

"Yeah, Ori. Let's get you in the sunshine," Carl says as he wraps an arm around Ori's waist.

Ori shoves Carl's arm off. A few seconds later, she wraps her arm around Carl's waist. *Oh, for fuck's sake. What a brat.*

"Fine. Allow us to exchange phone numbers and we'll get on the road," Ori says.

A few minutes later, we're in the car and on the way home. Ori is in the front seat, soaking up the sun and telling me about her ideas for future road trips. Carl is in the back looking up potential hotels to stay at tonight. Aside from Ori being a woman, everything is back to normal.

"We could teach Carl to drive if the new identification works for him, make the trips easier on you," Ori says.

"By *we* you mean *me*," I laugh.

"Of course, darling. Oh! We could go to Orlando. I'm sure you'd enjoy seeing the theme parks."

"Ori, I'd rather stay in the house forever than be crowded together with a bunch of sweaty people at a theme park."

"As long as you're in the house with me then I'm happy."

"Okay, found one. Nine-point-five on the cleanliness scale and has an opening today," Carl says.

"Alright then. Load it into the GPS."

We get there in the evening. By then I'm absolutely beat. When we get to the room, I'm too tired to even do most of my preparations. I just check the mattress, strip off the comforter, and lay face down on a pillow.

"Are you okay, Anne?" Carl asks as he sits at the end of the bed.

"Yes. But my back hurts from so much driving and I'm just tired." I stretch my body, my joints making loud popping sounds.

"My poor Anne," Ori says as she climbs onto the bed. "You need a massage."

Ori straddles my hips and settles herself, using my ass as her seat.

"Hey now. I know what your massages lead to," I grumble.

"Oh, but I'm a different woman now. Just relax."

The back rub does feel great, I gotta admit. Especially my lower back. Driving for so long—

I moan as Ori slides down, lifts my skirt, and begins to rub my ass. The muscles there were apparently in great need of a massage. I'm just absolutely lost in the feeling when she starts to rub my inner thighs. *Here we go.* Just as expected Ori slides under my panties and starts to massage my clit with one hand. I can't help but to arch my back a little and follow her moves with my hips.

"Mm. You do love grinding on your pillow, don't you?" Ori says and I can practically hear the smirk in her voice.

I open my mouth to make a comeback, but Carl speaks before me.

"Take them off of her." The bed sinks as Carl lays down next to me. I turn to face him and find his pupils blown out with lust as he watches Ori fondle me.

"Say please," Ori hisses.

"Please. Take them off." Carl unzips his jeans.

"Anything for you, little fishy," Ori says as she slides my panties down my legs.

I take the opportunity to turn over onto my back before she can stop me. Ori gives me a wry look. Carl places his hand on my cheek and brings our faces close together.

"Kiss me, Anne," he whispers. Of course I do—there are few things I love more in the world than kissing Carl. And I know he loves kissing me. If I didn't know it, I would now, considering he's rubbing his cock while we do it. I pull away from the kiss for a second to watch him stroke himself. It's a thing of beauty. He pulls me back to him and we kiss more.

"Kissing without me?" Ori sighs.

I reach my hand in her general direction until she takes it. A gentle tug has her climbing my body until she's back straddling my hips. Ori kisses behind my ear, then down my neck. When she gets to my chest, she lifts the t-shirt over my breasts, then slips each one out of the bra cups. I'm sure I look crazy at this point with my skirt hiked up to my belly button and my shirt like this; and I'm pretty sure I lost a sock at some point. When Ori starts sucking on my nipple, reaches between her legs to start rubbing my clit again, I stop thinking about clothes entirely.

"I think we need to do a more thorough massage, hmm?" Ori says before spreading my thighs wide apart. "Yes, I'm sure that will help you relax."

I turn away from Carl to speak to her.

"Take off your clothes. I want to see you," I say.

Ori stills, body language wary. "Are you sure?"

"Yes. Let me see."

After a pause, Ori climbs off of me and onto the floor where she stands awkwardly. She lifts her black shirt over her head with a resigned sigh. Next, she unzips her matching skirt and lets it fall to the floor, then pulls her lacy panties down. I take in her new, temporary appearance. She's stunning. I've never been with a woman before, but if I'm going to be with one, I feel incredibly blessed that it's one this gorgeous. Perky little breasts, flat stomach, long legs—pretty much the opposite of me, but somehow exactly how I would expect Ori to look.

"You're so beautiful. You look like a doll," I say as I run a hand down her thigh.

"Enough about me," Ori says as she climbs back onto the bed and makes herself at home between my thighs. Her eyes shine with desire as she kisses up my inner thigh. She licks up my center with a moan matching mine. "It's so good to be back."

I run my fingers through Ori's hair as she goes down on me, her pace slow, all the soft little sounds she makes telling me she's taking her time to enjoy this. Carl takes off his shirt so he can press against me skin-to-skin as we kiss.

Ori lifts her head and huffs out a quiet laugh. "Come on Carl, one more time before I change back, hmm?"

Carl breaks our kiss with a wide grin. He wiggles his eyebrows, making me giggle, before diving to the end of the bed. It takes me a second to realize what's going on, but when Carl lines himself up behind the bent-over Ori, it's pretty clear.

Ori and I lock eyes as Carl inserts himself into her. Her eyelids flutter as she clenches her teeth. The sight of my strong, golden man with his cock inside my beautiful woman is enough to have me reaching down to touch myself. Ori stops my hand with a growl.

"Absolutely not," she bites out before going back to work on me.

The rhythm of Carl pounding into her as she fucks me with her fingers and sucks on my clit has my head spinning. It doesn't take long before I come. Ori smiles at me before going back to try for another one. I stop her, though.

"No. You," I pant out. "On top of Carl."

Ori and Carl reposition so that she can ride his cock while facing away from him. I get between their legs this time. *Maybe my back still hurts a little, but it's worth it.* As Ori and Carl fuck, I lick Ori's clit. Unsurprisingly, she tastes like cotton. I keep an eye on her expression to make sure I'm doing okay.

"You're doing so well, Anne. Lick my cunt while Carl fucks me with his big cock. You're immaculate."

Her encouraging words have me licking with renewed fervor. She grabs my hair and shoves me harder against her as she cries out, "Faster Carl!"

Carl holds tight to her hips as he fucks upwards into her. The expression on Ori's face turns tense just before she gasps. She clamps her thighs around my head and groans loudly as her orgasm tears through her. When her muscles relax I back away to slide something out of my mouth. *A feather.* Carl squeezes her hips tight as he comes next. I look at the place where they intersect and find more little feathers there. I sit up and wipe my face, discovering more down stuck to it. When Ori sighs and climbs off of Carl, she leaves behind a layer of feathers and cum coating Carl's cock.

Ori notices me looking at the downy mess she left behind. "Well, what did you think would happen?"

I break out in a fit of giggles. "Oh sorry, I didn't think about the fact that my girlfriend would come feathers that would get all stuck in my boyfriend's jizz. It's not a normal, everyday thought."

"Our everyday lives seem to come with a lot of surprises. A suspicious number of them involve Ori's feathers though, you gotta admit," Carl says as he heads for the shower.

I continue to laugh and even Ori manages a smile as she pulls me up against her. We snuggle happily until it's my turn to shower. After that I sleep like a baby.

Chapter Thirteen

Ori

The rest of our road trip was uneventful, thankfully. I soaked up enough sun to change myself back into my male form and still have plenty of energy leftover. When we got home, Anne insisted we wash everything we brought with us immediately in case of bugs. After that, she took an incredibly long shower.

I've had to go out every day, sit on a bench, and read while I take in sunlight. It's been several days since we got back, so I've had plenty of time to catch up on my research. I've been looking into what it would take to buy land and live away from the city. How much money I'd need to make to fund a more private lifestyle. The numbers are not looking great, but I believe I can reach them. I can do anything if it's for Anne and Carl.

"Excuse me, son. May I take a seat?" an elderly woman asks.

"Of course, ma'am. Please, rest." I scoot over to make room.

The woman sits quietly, watching the birds while I read. As I'm thinking more and more about how long it might take me to save up, my usual worries creep in. *Will they be alright? What if something happens to them before that?* This anxiety has me in a chokehold. I turn to the woman next to me. Perhaps an outsider has perspective.

"Pardon me," I say, "But I'm wondering how to deal with the fact that all my loved ones will die someday. As an elder, perhaps you have some insight?"

The lady looks at me with pinched eyebrows above her thick glasses. "Well, you're not much for small talk, I guess."

"No."

She chuckles and sits back further on the bench. "Well, you see dear, the key is to enjoy them while you have them."

"But I'm worried about them all the time. They're here now, but one day they'll be gone."

She smiles softly. "That's true. Someday we'll all be gone. It's hard to accept that, but you just have to. My husband died when we were only forty. I'm eighty now and I've never been with anyone since him. I'm waiting to see him again, even though I'm sure that sounds silly to a lot of people."

I take her fragile hand in mine. Living forty years without Anne and Carl seems impossible to me. I could never do something so difficult. This woman is clearly strong and wise.

"What if there isn't any seeing him again? What if when we die there's nothing else? I'll have lost them forever."

"Honey, if there's nothing after we die, then you won't know the difference." She squeezes my hand and leans close. "Every thought you waste worrying about them dying is one you're not using to think of ways to love them even better. You gotta face it—we're all gonna die someday. It's up to you how you spend your time before then."

She's only partially right because we're not all going to die, not at the same time, anyway. *They* will die. *I* won't. I want to stop worrying about them, and this wonderful woman is right that worrying does me no good. But then I'm still left with the knowledge that when something inevitably does happen to them, I'll be left all alone.

There's only one thing I can do.

A few days later, when Anne and Carl are at work, I tidy up the living room for Marlon's visit later today. When that's done, I sit on the sofa, adjust the cuffs of my shirt, and clear my throat.

"Oh my, I have an idea," I say to the empty room. "I am going to find a new way to make my darlings live forever. I certainly hope that bird lady doesn't come back and get angry with me."

I wait a moment, but nothing happens. *I'll try again.*

"I sure am tired of the sun. I think I'll go back to draining people again. Perhaps I'll kill that cashier at the drugstore down the street. She was rude to Anne and I could increase my powers enough to—"

The room goes silent, all of that extra noise from electronics and traffic gone. A crack of lighting and a rumble of thunder later, the woman is in my living room, leaning against my doorway.

"What are you trying to do, Ori? I'm busy, and already annoyed that you're back so soon. Make it quick. I can do worse than make you a pillow."

"Yes, thank you for your time, Ms. Bird-Death-lady. You see—"

She holds up a hand to silence me. A couple of chickadees poke their heads out from her elegantly embroidered sleeve before returning to hiding.

"It's Morana. My name."

"Lovely name!"

"Thank you. Now, get to the point."

"As you know, I don't have a normal life span. Well, I have decided that I would like to die." I hold my hands up and chuckle nervously. "Someday. Not now. Should have worked on my phrasing. Anyway, when Anne and Carl have both gone, I would like my life to end as well. I don't want to go on without them. The idea of an eternity grieving them is too much to bear. I can't do it myself, so I'm hoping you could possibly do me that favor?"

"But certainly you'd want to live on. Think of all the things you can see, the places you could go, with all of that time. Most would see it as a gift"

"None of that matters if they're not there with me. I am only alive because of Anne. Her essence led my spirit out of the void. Carl taught me how to fall in love. They are my everything. Forever without them would be a far worse fate than missing out on some sightseeing."

"But you may not ever see them again. What happens after death is unknown."

"Even to you?" I raise a brow.

"My case is special, and my story is long, Ori. But as far as what happens to regular humans? I have no idea."

"I still want it. Alternatively, you could make them live for—"

"Death it is," she laughs. "Call my name when you're ready to go. But make sure you're *really* ready. You never know what fate has in store for you. You could change your mind."

"Thank you, Morana."

"And don't piss me off in the meantime." She points her scythe at me. "I mean it."

"I will be on my best behavior."

"Mmhm." She stands up straight and waves one hand. "Until then, feather."

"Until death."

Later on, Carl comes home sprinting up the stairs and into the front door with an envelope in his hand and a smile on his face.

"Look what was in the mail," he says as he hands me the envelope.

I take out the items inside and set them on the coffee table. A passport, birth certificate, social security card, and a driver's license meant for Carl. They all look legitimate.

"This is a driver's license. You don't know how to drive," I say.

"I will when Anne teaches me."

"Oh boy," Anne says from the hall.

"Carl," I lean close to his ear. "I have some thoughts for tomorrow."

A short bit later, Marlon, Charlie, and Imani come over again for dinner. We're able to properly chat, this time. Unfortunately, I discover that I *do* like Marlon and I *am* glad to have him as a brother. I suppose he could come around occasionally. Even the child manages to get on my good side, somehow.

"Here, Imani. You with your dad in the back," I tell her as we're setting up for the family photo Anne insists on.

"Which dad?" she asks.

"Doesn't matter. Just don't make any silly faces. My Anne wants a nice photo, so you must behave."

"Uncle Ori," she says as she sets her little hand on my arm. She offers me a gravely serious expression. "I can't make any promises."

"I can't blame you," I say as I look over at my family. "Mischief is simply part of who we are, it would seem."

The next day, Anne and Carl join me for my daily sunshine. Carl walks ahead, Anne and I behind him.

"It's nice to get out of the office, ugh," Anne says.

"Yeah, it was a long week," Carl replies.

"Ori, can you please just tell us where you got the flame?" Anne asks. She asks every day.

I sigh. "Fine."

Carl and Anne both perk up.

"I searched forever until I found someone online who would meet me to sell me what I needed. It was expensive."

"That's not anything weird or embarrassing. Why didn't you just tell us?" Carl asks.

"There's more to the story. The person who sold it to me was the governor."

I'm convinced the man is a part of a secret alien worshipping cabal. Anne thinks it's an insane theory, but there are so many videos online discussing it. They can't all be wrong! And really, why would he have access to magic items if he wasn't involved in something strange? There's a mystery there I intend to solve someday.

"Uh, okay. I mean, I know you're weird about the government, so I suppose I could see why you were being secretive," Anne says with a shrug.

"There's one more thing. He took a shine to me and wanted...well, I also had to give him underwear as part of the deal."

"Oh, well, that's not that embarrassing? You normally work in the erotic transactions field, anyway. It's not that different. Is it? Well, selling your underwear is more intimate, I guess," Anne says.

"Calling my work *erotic transactions* makes it sound very frumpy, Anne, and I am far from that. Anyway, I didn't give him *my* underwear."

"Ori! Why didn't you ask before selling my underwear?" Anne asks in an angry tone.

"It wasn't your underwear either," I shrug.

After a few seconds, Carl pauses. "Wait, huh? Why me?"

"Well, I couldn't give him mine. They're made of *me*. It's far too risky."

"But I called the neighbor across the hall an underwear thief!"

I shove my hands into my pockets and look ahead. "Anyway, let's enjoy the lovely sunshine."

We walk quietly for several long blocks. A smile grows larger and larger on my face. Anne squints at me.

"What's going on with you?" she asks. "You're suspiciously quiet."

"Oh, I'm only enjoying our walk. Aren't the trees lovely this time of year?" I say as we begin down a path leading through the little woods near the park, Carl leading the way.

"I guess. Fall is more my thing," she shrugs.

"What do you think, Carl? When is the forest your favorite?"

He pauses to let us catch up, then stands on the opposite side of Anne. "It's my favorite whenever I'm with you."

Slowly, we veer further and further from the path. Shadows become more frequent than rays of light on the forest floor.

"Hey guys, we're pretty far into these trees. Let's turn around," Anne says.

"No, I don't think we will. Not yet," I say.

"We thought you might want to play a little game with us, Anne," Carl says.

The two of us stand behind her.

"What's going on?" Anne asks.

"All you have to do is run. We'll take care of the rest," Carl says softly against her neck.

"Run?"

"Yes, darling." I say with a kiss to her cheek.

"But I don't—"

I nip her earlobe hard enough to get her full attention, then drag my teeth down her neck. When she shudders, I growl softly into her ear. I can see her pulse racing. Lightly, I let my lips caress her ear as I whisper the word that sends her running.

"Go."

Thank You

♥

Thank you to everyone who has read the Stuffed books. You've changed my life in ways I can't even begin to explain. Writing this series, developing these characters, and sharing them with you has been a fantastic experience. I truly have the most wonderful readers in the world.

I also want to express my gratitude to everyone who has supported me along the way. I couldn't have done this without your help.

A special thank you to Tee and Alijay for assisting me with covers, promotions, stickers, and so many other tasks throughout this past year. You're amazing!

I'd also like to thank Latrexa and Cassie for "aggressively helping" me when I was ready to give up. A bouncing frog emoji to you.

Audiobooks, Etc.

♥

Audiobooks and More

You can find the audiobooks for Stuffed and Double Stuffed on Amazon, Audible, and iTunes today.

The Spanish version of Stuffed, *Repleta*, is now available on eBook at multiple retailers.

If you would like to order the paperback of Stuffed for your bookstore or library, it's currently available through Ingram.

Bubble Tea

♥

Want More Sentient Object Fun?

If you enjoyed Stuffed, you may enjoy my other sentient object romances, such as My Date with Bubble Tea.

You'll flip your lid for this bubble tea.

Adanna enjoys the sweet side of life: frilly clothes, adorable puppies, and walks in the fresh spring air are the thing for her. When she thinks she's spotted something else sweet to add to her collection—a gorgeous man sitting on a bench sipping a bubble tea—she struts over to get her guy.

Too bad a misfit fairy accidentally turns the man, Harry, into a bubble tea before she can get there!

Thankfully, she can change Harry back. But first, Adanna has to fall in love with him, boba and all. Then they have to prove that love—physically.

How are they supposed to fall in love when one of them is a cup of tea? And does his straw go *there* or not?